D1714361

Castaway Corpse

Lucy McGuffin, Psychic Amateur Detective Book 8

Maggie March

Chihuahua Publishing

Contents

Chapter One

THERE ARE TWO KINDS of people in this world: Muffin people and everybody else. The everybody else consists of the usual suspects—the cookie people, the cupcake people, and last but not least, the doughnut people.

Don't get me wrong. I have nothing against any of them personally. But my people are the muffin people. They're the ones who frequent The Bistro by the Beach, the café I co-own with my friend Sarah Powers here in Whispering Bay, Florida.

The muffin people totally get me. They also help keep me in business, so when one of my "people" asks for a favor, it's hard to say no.

Victor Marino, a retired postal worker and a regular here at the café, stands across the counter looking at me with pleading eyes and a story I'm finding hard to resist because it's just so deliciously out there.

"Let me get this straight," I say to Victor and his shifty seventy-something-year-old sidekick, Phoebe Van Cleave. "You want Paco to help you channel the ghost of some dead pirate?"

Phoebe and Victor belong to the Sunshine Ghost Society, a local group that likes to commune with the dead. A year ago, I would have laughed in their faces, but a lot has happened in the past twelve months that makes it impossible for me to remain skeptical.

Paco, who likes to hang out with me behind the counter while I'm working, gives me a look that lets me know he's just as intrigued by this dead pirate as I am. He's a tan chihuahua-terrier mix that I rescued after I solved a local murder. Since then, Paco and I have gone on to solve numerous crimes.

The majority of our sleepy little north Florida community attributes our sleuthing success to luck. But luck has nothing to do with it. Paco, you see, is a ghost whisperer, and I have the gift of knowing when someone is lying or telling the truth. Together, we're quite the dynamic duo.

Most people are aware of Paco's ghost-whispering abilities—he even has his own Facebook page that was set up by a former owner. But only family and a handful of my closest friends know about my special gift. On top of all that, Paco and I can now communicate with one another. It took me a while to figure it out, but he understands human language. We can also sense what the other one is thinking. Don't ask me how it works. It just does. At least, for now.

"Lucy," Victor says, "it's not just any dead pirate. It's Lazy Eye Louie!"

I can't help but snort. "Why can't pirates have normal names, like John Jones?"

Phoebe rolls her eyes at me like she's dealing with a nitwit. "Lazy Eye Louie was the nickname given to Luis Sánchez. Is *that* normal enough for you?"

I'd like to nit her wit. Phoebe Van Cleave has been a thorn in my side for as long as I've known her. If I say black, she says white. But I have to put up with her because as president of the Sunshine Ghost Society, she could easily choose to hold their weekly breakfast meetings at another café, and I'd hate to lose them as customers. Especially if they decided to hold their meetings at Heidi's Bakery, a local establishment that makes great pancakes and, yes, I'll admit it, even better doughnuts.

Recently, Heidi's Bakery got a five-spoon review from the Fussy Foodie, a notoriously picky food critic who writes a snarky blog. One good review from him and you're gold.

Not that I'm jealous or anything. No way! Why should I be jealous when I make the best muffins in the world (not that *I'd* say my muffins were the best in the world, but others have, and who am I to contradict them?).

Sarah and I have worked hard to make our café warm and inviting. The building sits on prime real estate overlooking the crystal-clear blue water of the Gulf of Mexico. The walls are painted with murals of frolicking dolphins, the floors are a polished light wood, and Jimmy Buffet can always be heard on the overhead speaker. Plus, the food is unbelievable.

If the Fussy Foodie had taken the time to visit The Bistro by the Beach, I'm sure we would have gotten a five-spoon review too.

I shake myself back to the conversation. "Luis Sánchez, huh? Never heard of him."

"He was rumored to have stolen a fortune in doubloons from another pirate before taking off on a boat that eventually crashed during a storm," says Victor. "His body, as well as any treasure he might have stolen, was never recovered." His eyes gleam with excitement. "Here's the good part. The pirate he stole the treasure from was none other than José Gaspar."

Most people in Florida know the legend of José Gaspar, an early nineteenth-century pirate who raided up and down the Florida west coast and hid out in the Tampa Bay. Heck, there's even a festival named after him.

Every winter, the streets of Tampa go wild on Gasparilla weekend, when basically the whole town turns into one big pirate fest. There's a boat flotilla, a parade, fireworks, and lots of drunken shenanigans. My one and only Gasparilla experience ended with me getting hit between the eyes by a bead missile that knocked my glasses clear off my face, so I've avoided it ever since.

"I thought José Gaspar wasn't real. I mean, isn't he just an excuse for people to behave badly?"

Phoebe raises a brow at me. "It's true. No historian has been able to verify his existence. Until *now,*" she adds dramatically. "With Paco's help, we could make one of the most important discoveries in recent history."

Paco barks. *Tell me more.*

Betty Jean Collins, who works part-time at the café, pops her head out the cutaway window connecting the kitchen to the dining area. Betty Jean is eighty but has the soul of a frustrated teenager in the throes of puberty. She's also a member of the Sunshine Ghost Society and almost as nosy as Phoebe. "Well?" she asks Victor and Phoebe like I'm not standing three feet from her face. "Is Lucy on board?"

"She's thinking about it," Victor says.

Sarah pokes her head around Betty Jean to see what's going on. Sarah is a few years older than me, blond, blue-eyed, and beautiful. She's also a terrific friend, a great business partner, and makes the best macaroni and cheese you've ever tasted. "What's up?" she asks, her gaze curious.

"Phoebe and Victor want Lucy's permission to use Paco during a séance to conjure up the ghost of Lazy Eye Louie," Betty Jean explains as if this scenario is all perfectly normal.

Sarah makes a face. "Sorry I asked."

I glance around the near-empty dining room. It's ten till two, which means it's almost closing time. "Let's sit down to talk about this. Betty Jean can man the counter in case someone comes in."

Betty Jean scurries to take my place, leaving me free to follow Victor and Phoebe to a table in the corner. Naturally, Paco trots along. I stretch out my back and have a seat. It's been a long day, and something tells me it's about to get even longer. "Okay, start from the beginning."

Victor nods eagerly. "I got a call this morning from Professor Mortimer Drake. Have you heard of him?"

"Sorry. The name doesn't ring a bell."

"He's written a book chronicling the history of piracy in Florida. Fascinating stuff. He's spent most of his career trying to prove the existence of José Gaspar."

Against my better judgment, I motion for him to continue.

"About a month ago, he stumbled across the diary of a bootlegger—a man by the name of Luis Sánchez."

"Also known as Lazy Eye Louie," I say, warming up to the nickname. I have to admit, it does have a certain panache to it.

"That's right," Victor says. "Before he was known as Lazy Eye, Luis was a Spanish soldier stationed in Cuba during the early nineteenth century who went AWOL. He stole a boat and sailed away to Florida. It's here that he met a pirate by the name of Jean Marquette—"

"Ooh. What was his pirate name?"

Victor blinks. "Um, he didn't have a pirate name. At least, none that I'm aware of."

"Oh." Well, that's disappointing. What's the point of being a pirate if you don't have a cool name?

"According to Sánchez's diary," Victor continues, "he began selling liquor to Marquette. And that's where things get interesting."

Paco nudges my leg with the tip of his cold nose. *I hope you're getting all this.*

Oh, brother. Who knew my dog had a pirate fetish?

"Interesting, how?"

"According to Sánchez's diary, Marquette was none other than José Gaspar's right-hand man. One night while they were drinking, Sánchez tricked Marquette into showing him where Gaspar hid his gold. Sánchez snuck back later and stole it."

"And we know this because of this lost diary of his?"

"Exactly," Phoebe says. "Historians believe that Lazy Eye Louie fled with another pirate's booty, only to have his boat sink during a storm. It was presumed that Lazy Eye Louie, along with the treasure, were somewhere at the bottom of the gulf. Until the discovery of the diary, they didn't know that the pirate he stole from was Gaspar."

"And how exactly does Paco work into this scenario?"

"There's an unexplored island approximately twenty miles off the coast of Whispering Bay. The island's coordinates put it in the very path that Lazy Eye Louie noted in his diary. It's a long shot, but Professor Drake has hired a crew to take him out to the island so he can explore. If the professor is right in his hunch, and he always is—the man is *absolutely* brilliant—this could be the clue to finding Lazy Eye Louie's remains."

Long shot? It sounds more like a wild goose chase to me.

"And you want to do a séance?" I ask. "After all these years, you'd think Louie would have moved on."

Phoebe makes a face. "Lucy McGuffin, how many times do I have to explain to you that the spirit tends to linger near the earthly body?"

"Yeah, yeah." I take it all in. "Let's say, as improbable as this sounds, Lazy Eye Louie's body is on that island and Paco is able to communicate with him. Then what?"

Victor leans in eagerly. "Then maybe he'll tell us the truth about José Gaspar. Can you imagine, Lucy, if we were the ones who could provide hard evidence that Gaspar was a real person? The Sunshine Ghost Society would be famous! They'll write articles about us in all the journals. We might even be on TV."

I'm not sure how the spirit of some long-ago dead pirate could provide any "hard evidence" of José Gaspar's existence, but past experience has taught me that where the Sunshine Ghost Society is concerned, logic flies out the door.

"Don't forget, Victor, we're not the only ones who would benefit from this," Phoebe points out. "All of Professor Drake's hard work would finally be recognized the way it should be."

The hair on the back of my neck tingles. It's the physical reaction I get whenever someone lies to me. The bigger the reaction, the bigger the lie. Only, this tingling sensation is so subtle that I barely noticed it.

Nothing in Phoebe's statement feels like a lie, but if it caused my Spidey sense to go off even the tiniest bit, there's something not quite right with what she's just said. It's as if Phoebe has a personal stake in this discovery beyond her ties to the Sunshine Ghost Society.

"So, this Professor Drake," I say to Phoebe, "you follow his work?"

Phoebe sniffs. "You forget, Lucy. Before I retired, I taught history at Whispering Bay High for over thirty years. Anyone with any interest in Florida history has read all of Mortimer Drake's books."

Lucky for me Phoebe had already retired by the time I hit high school. "When are you going out on the boat?" I ask.

"Saturday," Victor says. "We're leaving the marina at 8 a.m. sharp."

"That's tomorrow!"

Victor grimaces. "We only discovered all this today when Professor Drake reached out to our society to see if we could be of help. Naturally, Phoebe and I immediately thought of Paco."

Sometimes my dog's fame is a real pain in the rear end.

"I couldn't let him go out on a boat without me. And I'm working. Saturdays are always busy. Can't you get a human medium to help you? You must have a couple of those lying around somewhere."

"Actually, we are getting some help in that department," Victor says. "The medium's name is Bonnie Clark. She's flying in from New York just to be part of our expedition. She was recommended by a member of Dr. Drake's entourage, but her credentials are a bit sketchy. It would be so much better if we had someone we trusted, like Paco."

"Besides, one day away from this place isn't going to kill you," Phoebe says flippantly. "Sarah and Betty Jean will be here at The Bistro tomorrow, won't they? Not to mention that other person who helps out from time to time. What's her name again?"

"Jill!" Betty Jean yells from across the room. Boy, talk about mad skills. Betty Jean is either a master eavesdropper or she's got the best hearing aids in town.

"Don't you have your book club thing at the library tomorrow?" I shout back at her. Betty Jean runs a local book club that meets at her house once a month, and there's a waiting list to join. I'm an honorary member, but that's only because I bring free muffins to the meetings. Tomorrow, the book club members will be hosting a read-in at the library that's open to the public. It's a new program the library is trying out in an effort to show how reading can bring people together.

"It's not until noon, so I can work until eleven thirty. And no worries! I'll get Jill to cover for me," she shouts back.

"The Sunshine Ghost Society would be willing to pay Jill's wages if that would help free you up." Phoebe's beady eyes narrow. "You wouldn't want to rob Paco of this opportunity, would you?"

Paco looks up at me with his big brown chihuahua eyes. *Yes, yes, yes. I want to talk to a dead pirate.*

I feel like that parent who can't say no to her child even when they know they should. I've let the Sunshine Ghost Society use Paco as a medium before, and the results were almost disastrous. The society accidentally conjured up the ghost of a woman who'd kidnapped Paco, and it nearly cost me my precious little dog. I'm not sure I'm willing to take that risk again. No matter how intriguing this pirate adventure sounds.

Victor hands me a slip of paper. "Here's all the information you'll need regarding the boat, the island, and the departure time." He spears me with a look almost as pathetic as Paco's. "Please, Lucy. It would mean the world to us."

"Let me think about it," I say.

Paco barks happily. *Oh goody. That means yes.*

Chapter Two

"FOR YOUR INFORMATION," I say to my dog, giving him the stern face (so that he knows I mean business), "the phrase *let me think about it* does not mean yes."

Paco makes a petulant *pfft* sound under his breath. We're sitting on the couch in the living room in my apartment above The Bistro watching our favorite TV show, *America's Most Vicious Criminals*. It's a Friday night tradition that includes my best friend, Will Cunningham, cold beer, and pepperoni pizza from Tiny's Pizza—the best 'za joint in town. Tonight, we're joined by my boyfriend, Travis Fontaine, Travis's dog, Ellie, and my other best friend, Brittany Kelly.

It's a perfect way to end a busy work week, and even though I still have to wake up at four in the morning to bake the muffins, I never miss the ending to the show because that's when you find out the fatal clue that led the cops to the killer.

Brittany's eyes are glued to the TV screen. "Do you think the apartment manager is in on it? He seems shifty to me."

Not to toot my own horn or anything, but I ruled out the apartment manager within the first three minutes of the show. Still, I hate to come across as a know-it-all and hurt Brittany's feelings.

I reach for another slice of pizza. "Good point. He does seem pretty cagey."

Brittany and I grew up together, and while we were never friends in school, she's become my closest female confidant. She has a huge crush on Will. Not that I blame her. I used to crush on Will too before Travis came to town. Growing up, Will used to be my brother Sebastian's best friend, but he became my best friend too when he saved me from a pack of ravenous squirrels on my seventh birthday.

About a year ago, Brittany and Will went out on a much-anticipated date, and while Brittany thought the date went smashingly (she's optimistic like that), Will has fought any attempts to get the two of them together again.

The worst part about the whole thing is that he won't tell me why. I've thought about pressing him and trying to catch him in a lie so I can work it out, but whenever I bring up the subject of Brittany, Will tells me to "leave it alone, Lucy."

I'd love to see my two best friends as happy as Travis and me. Travis thinks I should respect Will's feelings and let Will and Brittany figure things out on their own. Ha! As if I'd leave something as important as true love to be "figured out on its own." If it were up to men, the world would be a lonely place.

Paco lays his head on my lap. *When are you going to decide if we can go on the pirate trip?*

"When I feel like it," I say to him.

Travis tears his gaze from the screen. "Lucy, are you talking to your dog again?"

"Yep." I pop a piece of pepperoni into my mouth. "He really wants to go on this crazy pirate ghost adventure, but I'm not so sure it's a good idea."

Travis shakes his head at me. Partly in amazement, and partly because I think he's still in disbelief. Did I mention that my boyfriend is Whispering Bay's chief of police? Like most cops, Travis prefers to deal in cold, hard facts, so it's been hard for him to accept that I have special skills, let alone that Paco and I can communicate with one another. But he's slowly getting used to the idea. Brittany and Will, on the other hand, adjusted just fine to the fact that their best friend is a human lie detector and her dog is a ghost whisperer.

"Wait." Will sits up straight. "Did you just say *pirate ghost adventure?*"

Everyone turns to look at me.

I brace myself. "Phoebe Van Cleave and Victor Marino want Paco and me to help this famous expert talk to the spirit of some dead pirate. All in the hopes of proving that José Gaspar was real."

At first, no one says anything. Then the room explodes with questions and they drag it all out of me, and now all they want to talk about is Lazy Eye Louie and if I'm going to let Paco go on the expedition.

Travis is against the idea because of course he is. As a police officer, he's naturally suspicious and sees danger lurking behind every corner. But Will is just as enthralled by the whole pirate mystique as Paco. And Brittany wants to know if there's an angle to this expedition that could increase tourism. She's the PR and marketing person for the Whispering Bay Chamber of Commerce, so she's always looking for ways to help the local economy.

Ellie makes a whining sound from her spot on the floor next to the couch. Travis bends down to pat her on the head. Ellie is a gorgeous German Shepherd who worked as a police dog for years before she was retired. Travis, along with the rest of the force, thought she'd lost her sense of smell. But boy, did she prove them wrong when not too long ago she single-handedly sniffed out a murder weapon that helped me solve a crime.

Ever since then, Travis has been taking Ellie to work with him. She's smart, obedient, and doesn't have a big attitude like some *other* dog I know. Paco was jealous of her at first, but over the past few months he and Ellie have become friends.

Will pulls out his cell phone. "Let me see what I can find out about this Professor Drake."

As our town's head librarian, Will believes in researching everything. He's also a highly successful author of espionage novels that he writes under the penname J.W. Quicksilver, but my brother Sebastian and I are the only ones in town who know this. For various reasons, Will wants to keep it strictly hush-hush.

Brittany smiles at Will like he's a judge at the Miss Cheese Grits Competition, a title she easily won back in her post-high-school beauty pageant days. It's an era in her life that she's put firmly behind her. Not that she couldn't still hop on a stage and win one of those things. At twenty-seven, Brittany is even more attractive now than she was in college. Her shoulder-length auburn hair always looks as if it's just been professionally styled, and she has the prettiest brown eyes ever. I have brown eyes too, but Brittany's eyes *twinkle*. I'd love to know how she manages that.

I used to be jealous of Brittany, but it's hard not to like someone who's literally put her neck out for you time and time again. I'll never have Brittany's beauty-queen looks. My brown curly hair has a mind of its own, and I like my muffins too much to ever be a size two or even a size eight. But you know what? Travis likes me just the way I am.

I like him just the way he is too. Which is no hardship because the man is the spitting image of Ryan Reynolds, has a heart of gold, and makes my girl parts do the hula just by looking at me. Unfortunately, he's also as stubborn as a goat. But hey, I'm no prize in that department either.

Travis points to Will's phone. "Find anything interesting?"

Will's gaze quickly scrolls through the screen. "It appears that this Professor Drake has written several books about the history of piracy in Florida. The reviews from academia are mixed."

"Meaning?" I ask.

Will shrugs. "It could mean anything, but the guy's background seems legit. He's got a PhD from The University of Florida and even spent a few years on their faculty."

I take the phone from Will's hand to have a look at this Dr. Drake. His long gray hair, pulled back in a low ponytail, combined with a strong chin, tweed suit and bow tie, create a dashing appearance. All he needs is a fedora and he could pass for the AARP version of Indiana Jones. "He certainly looks dashing enough."

"Just think," says Brittany, "if Professor Drake can prove the existence of José Gaspar, it could put Whispering Bay on the map." Her brown eyes twinkle even brighter.

Brittany has a point. This could be terrific for The Bistro by the Beach. Not that we don't already do a brisk business, but this could be the tipping point that allows us to expand. Or maybe even branch out into another café. As I scroll through the screen finding more articles about Professor Drake, my brain buzzes with possibilities. Then I read something that sends me crashing back down to earth.

"Oh no," I groan.

"What?" says Travis.

"Here's an article about the lost diary of Luis Sánchez. The one that Professor Drake just discovered tying him to José Gaspar. It says that the doubloons he stole from Gaspar are cursed."

Will chuckles. "Isn't all pirate gold cursed? And I prefer calling him Lazy Eye Louie. Luis Sánchez sounds too ordinary."

Brittany has the good sense to look concerned. "What else does is say, Lucy?"

"Not much, except that the diary is in the process of being authenticated by a panel of experts." I think back to the last time Paco was involved with a séance. "What if this Lazy Eye Louie transfers his bad juju to my dog?"

"Curse or no curse," Will says, "I think we should do it."

"We?" I say.

"Sure. We should all go. That way we can take turns keeping an eye on Paco." I can practically see the cogs in Will's brain spinning. I'm sure he sees some future book plot in all this, but my first responsibility is ensuring my little dog's safety.

I give Will a look. "I thought you had that big thing at the library tomorrow."

Brittany turns in the sofa to face him. "What big thing?"

"Betty Jean's book club is hosting an event. It's part of a new community outreach to get people excited about reading," he says without any enthusiasm, and I know why.

"That's fantastic," Brittany says. "But you should have told me. I could have promoted it on the chamber of commerce website."

I discreetly cough. "They're going to be reading the first chapter of J.W. Quicksilver's latest book, *Assassin's Code*. I hear it just made the *New York Times* bestseller list."

Travis nods absentmindedly, his eyes still glued to the TV screen. "I downloaded it onto my iPad last night. I'm already on chapter four. I think it's Quicksilver's best yet."

Will sinks into the couch. "You'd think a public library would have a more notable author to promote than this Quicksilver character."

It always unnerves me to hear Will talk about his alter ego this way. In some bizarre attempt to throw suspicion off himself, he always publicly dogs his own books. I think he's played the role of the snobby librarian for so long it's become second nature to him.

"Oh, I agree," Brittany says. "J.W. Quicksilver's books are just *awful*."

Will nods glumly. "It's no big deal. I can get Julie or any one of the other librarians to run the group."

"I don't know," I say. "This expedition is all so last-minute."

Paco barks to get my attention. *Hey! Don't I get a vote?*

"Not exactly, mister," I say to him, "I'm still the boss of you, and don't you forget it."

"What would you rather do," says Will, "work at the café on your feet for eight hours or spend a nice relaxing day on an island communing with nature?"

Boy, he's selling this hard. Will sees me wavering. "C'mon, Lucy! It'll be fun. And I promise, I won't take my eyes off Paco. I won't let anything happen to him."

"If Will goes, then I'll go," Brittany offers. "I can help watch Paco too."

It seems churlish of me to keep fighting this, especially when my two best friends have just volunteered to tag along.

We all turn to Travis, who, as usual, looks grim whenever someone suggests anything exciting. "Tomorrow is the annual police fitness exam, and I have to be at the station until five." He gives me a sideways look. "Plus, we have a reservation for dinner tomorrow at The Harbor House. Did you forget?"

Oops. Brittany's daddy owns The Harbor House, so naturally it's the fanciest restaurant in town. Their grilled grouper and cheese grits are to die for. My dress has been pressed and hung up in the closet ever since Travis made the reservation two weeks ago, so I didn't totally forget. I just sort of forgot that it was tomorrow night.

I lean over to give Travis a peck on the cheek. "I didn't forget, but the reservation is for seven. Right? According to Victor, we should be back by five, so I'll have plenty of time to get ready for our date."

Travis looks unconvinced. "If you want my opinion, I don't think it's a good idea to go."

"Why not?" Will challenges.

"Because we all know Lucy and Paco have a way of landing in trouble. Add in those wackos from the Sunshine Ghost Society, and it's a recipe for disaster. Besides," he adds, "has Paco ever been on a boat? What if he gets seasick? How are you going handle it?"

I hadn't thought of that. "Do dogs get seasick?"

"Let's find out." Will takes his phone back. He scrolls through several websites until something catches his attention, causing him to frown. Brittany peers over his shoulder. They exchange a terse look.

"What is it? Does it say dogs can get really seasick?"

"Uh, sure, but it's no worse than being in a car," Will says.

My scalp tingles. Will has just lied to me.

Paco barks loudly. *Not going to get sick. Want to go.*

Brittany rubs Paco behind the ears. "What's he saying, Lucy?"

"Paco says he wants to go."

Will jumps on this. "If Paco is willing to chance getting seasick, then I say yes. Besides, we can give him medicine. It says here he can have Dramamine. Just a small dose to prevent him from getting sick."

Paco cocks his head in that cute dog way and tries to melt me with his goo-goo eyes.

If I say no, he'll never let me forget it. And Will makes a good point. This could be fun. When I am to going to get the chance to tag along an expedition looking for the remains of an infamous dead pirate? And with both Will and Brittany helping me keep tabs on Paco, my dog should be safe.

But best of all, it's just occurred to me that *this* is the opportunity I've been waiting for. I've been thinking of a way to get Brittany and Will alone so he can realize how great the two of them can be together, and what's more together than spending a day on a deserted island?

"Okay, let's do it." I look over at Ellie, who stares back at me with her serious German shepherd eyes. I wish I knew what she was thinking, but my dog communication skills only work with Paco. "What about Ellie? Can we take her along?"

"Not gonna happen," Travis says.

"Why not? You know I'll take good care of her. Right? And with her sniffing skills, she'd be a great addition to the expedition."

His gaze softens. "I know you'll take good care of her. But what if she gets seasick? Do you really want a dog her size getting sick all over the boat? What if you have to deal with two sick dogs?"

"Not a problem. I have a cast-iron stomach."

"Sorry, Lucy, but she's helping me with the officer skills test. Isn't that right, girl?" He gives his dog a sloppy smile that warms me all the way down to my toes. How can you not love a man who loves his dog so much?

Ellie barks like she understands what he's saying, only I know she's just responding to the tone of his voice.

"So we're really doing this?" Will asks. "The four of us—you, me, Paco and Brittany? We're joining the Sunshine Ghost Society on Professor Drake's expedition tomorrow?"

"Yep. We're really doing this."

"Yes!" Will pumps his fist in the air. "You'll see, Lucy. This is gonna be great."

Chapter Three

EVEN THOUGH I'M TAKING the day off to go on a dead pirate expedition, I still wake up at four to make the muffins because my first responsibility is to The Bistro and to my customers.

Sarah and Betty Jean arrive at the café a little after five. Chances are, Betty Jean knows everything already, but in case she missed any details while eavesdropping, I tell them all I know about Lazy Eye Louie and his possible link to José Gaspar, as well as the ramifications of what it could mean for the Sunshine Ghost Society.

"This is so exciting!" Sarah says. "You and Paco definitely have to go."

Paco looks up at Sarah and wags his tail—the dog equivalent of a human smile.

"And you're okay with me taking the day off? Because I don't want to leave you shorthanded."

Betty Jean flutters a negligent hand through the air. "No worries. I've got that covered. I called Jill last night, and she's more than happy to fill in for you."

"I took last weekend off, so I owe you," Sarah says. "Besides, I'm dying of curiosity. If this Lazy Eye Louie really did end up on some island near Whispering Bay, it could be great for the local tourist economy."

"That's what Brittany thinks."

Betty Jean fluffs her bottle-bleached-blond hair. "I'm already putting together my wench outfit for the first annual Whispering Bay Pirate Festival."

Sarah and I exchange an amused look. I'm pretty sure we've both just visualized Betty Jean's idea of a costume. It would be worth finding Lazy Eye Louie's remains just to see Betty Jean decked out as a saucy pirate wench.

"Let's not get ahead of ourselves," I say. "First, we have to find proof that Lazy Eye Louie ended up somewhere near that island. Then we have to get Paco to communicate with his spirit. Even if all that were to happen, we'd still need to get evidence that José Gaspar actually existed."

"What about Sánchez's diary?" asks Betty Jean. "Isn't that evidence enough?"

"The diary is still being authenticated."

"You mean it could be fake?" Sarah looks taken aback. "Why would someone create a fake diary? What's in it for them?"

"Who knows? This is my first pirate rodeo."

"Oh, I know all about pirates," Betty Jean says. "They're my favorite to role-play."

Sarah blinks. "Role-play?"

"Sure, you know. In the bedroom. I used to be into the whole Jon Snow and Daenerys thing from *Game of Thrones,* but that got old fast." Betty Jean wags her brows up and down suggestively. "Pirates are a lot spicier, if you know what I mean."

Ugh. I cover Paco's ears with the palms of my hands. "Not in front of the dog," I hiss. Not only has Betty Jean ruined *Game of Thrones* forever, but now the image of her dressed as a saucy pirate wench has taken on a whole new meaning.

Betty Jean shakes her head at me. "You're no fun."

Paco barks like he agrees with her.

"Hey, I could still change my mind about going on this pirate adventure," I warn my dog.

Paco looks sufficiently chastised. I almost open my mouth to say, "That's better," but I'm smart enough to quit while I'm ahead.

A knock at The Bistro door startles us all. I glance over to see Heidi Burrows behind the glass pane waving at us. "Yoo-hoo! Lucy! It's me, Heidi!"

As if I couldn't tell. I've only known her all my life.

I go to unlock the door. "Hey, there. We don't open for another hour," I tell Heidi, who knows darn good and well our hours of operation because they're the same hours her bakery is open.

Heidi laughs. "Well, of course not."

"Shouldn't you be making doughnuts?" I ask. Then I notice that she's wearing a light blue dress and heels. Her blond hair is pulled up in a smart-looking 'do, and she's wearing makeup. Heidi is in her thirties, and she's attractive enough. I suppose.

"Oh, Lucy, you'll never believe it! I'm driving over to Pensacola to film a segment for one of the cable morning shows. *Good Morning, North Florida*. You've heard of it, right?"

I grit my teeth and nod.

"They found out about my five-spoon review from the Fussy Foodie and they want to interview me. Can you believe it? Naturally, I can't show up to the studio empty-handed. I brought boxes of my doughnuts for the crew, and I was almost out of town when I thought, why shouldn't I spread the love? I was thinking I could bring a box of your muffins. Who knows? Maybe someone will fall in love with them the way the Fussy Foodie fell in love with my doughnuts. We bakers have to stick together!"

"That's so ... thoughtful of you."

She smiles and waits expectantly. I have no choice but to give her a box of my very best muffins. Naturally, they're all delicious. That goes without saying. But comparing doughnuts to muffins just isn't fair. My muffins weren't made to put people into cholesterol shock. Not like Heidi's fat-laden sugar-bomb slabs of fried dough.

She takes the box and waves to Sarah and Betty Jean on her way out the door. "Wish me luck, ladies!"

Maybe *someone* will fall in love with my muffins the way the Fussy Foodie fell in love with her doughnuts?

Of all the nerve. I always knew Heidi had an ego the size of Alaska.

I take a deep cleansing breath. It's a beautiful bright Florida morning with lots of sunshine. A perfect day to be out on the water and forget all about Heidi, her doughnuts, and most importantly, the Fussy Foodie.

Paco and I arrive at the dock thirty minutes before the boat is scheduled to leave. My cell phone buzzes. It's Molly McGuffin, aka Mom.

"Hey, Mom, I don't have time to talk right now," I say, walking toward the dock.

"Why? Because you're about to get on a boat to who knows where to search for a dead pirate?"

I'm not even going to ask her how she knows about this.

"Good to know the grapevine is alive and well in Whispering Bay."

"Your father ran into Victor Marino last evening at the Piggly Wiggly, and he said it's all Victor could talk about." There's a pause. "I thought Travis was taking you to The Harbor House tonight for dinner."

"This expedition should be over by five so I'll have plenty of time to get ready for dinner."

Mom sounds unconvinced. "You should be relaxing today! Not running around on some deserted island. I was hoping we could get mani-pedis. You know, like regular mothers and daughters."

I'm not going to lie. The idea of a pedicure sounds heavenly right now.

"How about later next week? But remember, you have to make the appointment after two, when The Bistro closes."

"Next week is too late."

"Too late for what?"

"Nothing," she mutters.

A tingling sensation runs down the back of my neck. Mom isn't lying, but she's definitely hiding something. Knowing Mom, though, it could be anything.

"Why don't you call Sebastian and ask him to go with you?"

Mom scoffs. "Don't be ridiculous."

"Why? Because he's a man? Or because he's a priest? Men get pedicures too, you know." My older brother Sebastian is the pastor at St. Perpetua's Catholic Church here in town. He's also the busiest person I know, so this is probably a moot point.

Mom sighs heavily. "Forget I mentioned it."

"Will do. Gotta go!"

"Wait. Promise me you'll call if anything happens."

"Like what?"

"Like … anything."

"Okay, I promise." I hang up before she can make any more excuses to keep me on the line. I'm pleased to find Brittany and Will are already waiting on the dock.

"Did you two drive over in the same car?" Because if they did, maybe I don't have quite so much work to do in the matchmaking department.

"No, I just got here," Will says, bursting my bubble. He gives Brittany a side look. "Hey."

"Hey," she says brightly. She's wearing white cotton jeans cuffed to just below her knees, a navy blue and white striped shirt, and slip-on sneakers. Her hair is French-braided, and she's sporting an adorable white sailor hat. It's like she just stepped off the cover of a yachting magazine.

I opted for comfort—baggy shorts and a T-shirt that reads *Fear The Muffin Top*. It's an oldie but goodie. The day this T-shirt dies in the wash, a little piece of me will die along with it.

Will pulls off his sunglasses. "What's the name of the boat?"

"I'm not sure." I dig out a sheet of paper from my shorts pocket. "This is what Victor gave me yesterday. It says the boat is in spot number four."

Scanning the docked vessels, I spy a large boat anchored at the end of the long dock. It's the only boat that looks big enough to hold more than a few people. "That must be it down there." Will follows my gaze with interest.

Brittany peeks inside my bag. "It looks like you've got everything except the kitchen sink in there."

"Pretty much." I'm not about to go out to sea for a full day without essential supplies. That includes a doggie life jacket and food for Paco, sunscreen, bottled water, assorted snacks (okay, mainly muffins) and toilet paper (in case the boat has the cheap one-ply kind). And last but not least, the Dramamine.

Brittany pulls out the bottle. "Is this the seasick medicine?"

I nod. "I wasn't sure whether to give it to Paco with his breakfast this morning. It says it could make him sleepy. I hate to wait until he's actually sick to give it to him, but I also hate to give him medication that he might not need. If I'd had more warning, I could have gotten something from Dr. Brooks," I say, referring to Paco's veterinarian. "This is meant for humans, but I read on the internet that it's okay to give to dogs."

"What do you think?" Brittany hands the bottle to Will.

Will reads the label, then looks out toward the gulf like he's trying to figure out how choppy the water might get. "I say we give him the lowest dose. Just in case. That shouldn't make him too sleepy. We don't want the little guy to get sick if we could have helped him."

"Good idea. The recommended dose online was two to four milligrams per pound."

"How much does he weigh?" he asks.

"He's fifteen pounds."

Paco grunts. *Fourteen point seven ounces to be exact.*

"They rounded it up, okay?" Apparently, he's still bitter about his last vet check. Dr. Brooks is always admonishing me to keep Paco's weight down, but it's hard not to sneak him a bite of muffin every now and then.

Will studies the bottle again. "These are fifty mg tablets." He pulls out a pill and snaps it in half. "This should be about twenty-five mg, so it's an even lower dose than suggested. I think we'll be okay giving him that." He places the broken pill in the palm of his hand and offers it to my dog. Paco takes a few disinterested sniffs, then turns his head away.

"Paco," I say, "this pill will help keep you from getting sick on the boat."

Don't want it.

Ugh. I take the pill from Will's hand and try to stuff it down Paco's mouth, but he fights me, thrashing his head around and making a big production. He pulls this same routine every month when I give him his heart and flea medication. If dogs qualified for an academy award, Paco would win hands down.

Finally, I get the pill on the back of his tongue. Before he can react, I hold his jaws together, trying to force him to swallow it. We stare at one another in the age-old classic showdown between a stubborn pet and his owner.

"Poor thing," Brittany says. "He must have swallowed it by now, don't you think?"

"Trust me, he hasn't swallowed it." I narrow my eyes at Paco. "If you're holding out for some peanut butter or applesauce, you can forget it. I don't have any with me."

How about some muffin?

I knew it! No way am I going to let my dog blackmail me.

I let go of his jaw. He easily spits the pill out onto the dock. *No muffin. No pill.*

"Fine by me." I toss the bottle of Dramamine back inside my bag. "Don't blame me when you're barfing all over the ship deck."

Paco turns up his nose. *I have too much dignity for that.*

Dignity, huh? When did my dog learn such big words? I hope for his sake, he's right. This is supposed to be a fun adventure, and cleaning up doggie vomit isn't my idea of a good time.

Chapter Four

"Lucy!" At the sound of Victor's voice, I turn to see him and Phoebe heading down the dock. They're accompanied by a woman I've never seen before. She must be Bonnie Clark, the medium who flew into town for today's expedition.

"I knew you'd come," Victor says, beaming. He turns to Phoebe. "Didn't I tell you? Lucy and Paco wouldn't let us down."

Phoebe takes one look at Will and Brittany. "What are they doing here?" she demands.

Victor looks like he's swallowed a frog. "I didn't think it would be a problem. I ran into Brittany last night and she—"

"They're coming with us, and that's final," I say.

"Lucy," Phoebe says as if Will and Brittany aren't right in front of her, "we can't invite the whole town. Practically everyone in the society wanted to be a part of this expedition, but obviously that can't happen. The only reason Bonnie is here is because of her skills as a medium. She'll be assisting Paco and acting as his translator, helping put his thoughts into words for the rest of us."

Considering that I know what Paco is thinking, I could easily play that role, except then everyone would know I have supernatural skills, and I certainly don't want to open up that can of worms.

"Right. But if you want Paco, then Will and Brittany are a package deal. Sorry, but that's nonnegotiable."

Phoebe bristles at the smugness in my voice. It's not often I get the upper hand on Phoebe Van Cleave. Speaking of which, she looks exceptionally nice today. In appearance only, mind you, but she's definitely upped her game. Normally, she pulls her salt-and-pepper hair back in a bun and opts for practical shorts or jeans, but today she's wearing a sundress with sandals, and she's styled her hair into a smooth chin-length bob. She's even put on lipstick. Huh. What gives?

Before Phoebe can open her trap, Bonnie wisely jumps in. She's in her mid-forties, which makes her about two decades younger than the average Sunshine Ghost Society member. "Lucy McGuffin! It's great to finally meet you! I simply *adore* your muffins," she gushes, pumping my hand up and down. Strawberry-blond hair peeks out from the edge of her head scarf, and the skin at the corners of her hazel eyes crinkles, giving her a slightly mischievous look.

Funny, I've never seen Bonnie before in my life. Phoebe said she just flew in from New York, so I can't imagine how she's tasted my muffins. Maybe she dropped by The Bistro this morning after I left?

"Thank you. I'm sorry, I don't recall seeing you in the café. Phoebe said you're from New York?"

"I was in Whispering Bay a couple of months ago, just for a day or so, and I had a chance to drop by your charming little restaurant then."

I'm not picking up any telltale signs of her lying, so I'll have to take this at face value. "Which muffin is your favorite?" I ask, not because I'm looking for more praise or anything, but it's important to know these sorts of details.

"Oh, that's easy. The coffee cake supreme."

Interesting choice. The coffee cake supreme is the love child of my mother's coffee cake recipe and my cinnamon swirl muffin. It's my latest creation, but I'm still tweaking the recipe. If the current version is her favorite, she'll be blown away (as will everyone else) when I achieve the final product.

"You know, Lucy, I love to putter around the kitchen. Not that my baking skills come anywhere close to yours, but I do consider myself a bit of a foodie. From one fellow baker to another, what's your secret for making the coffee cake supreme muffin so moist?"

I hesitate to answer, but what the heck. "Sour cream."

Her eyes widen. "Really? I'd *love* to have the recipe."

Mmm ... That's going a bit too far. I mean, you wouldn't expect Picasso to give away free art lessons, would you? Still, I have to give her credit for trying. I smile blandly. "We'll see."

Her gaze goes to Paco. "I've heard that your dog is an incredibly talented medium. I'm looking forward to seeing him in action." She bends down and scratches Paco behind the ears.

"Paco's incredible, all right."

He wags his tail. *You better believe it.*

I have no idea where my dog gets this ego of his.

Victor checks his wristwatch. "Do you think Professor Drake is already on the boat?" he asks Phoebe.

Before Phoebe can answer, Will points back toward the marina. "Looks like that's him over there."

We spin around to get our first glimpse of the infamous Mortimer Drake. He looks exactly like his photo, only instead of the tweed suit and bow tie, he's sporting Bermuda shorts and flip-flops, as well as a baseball cap with a University of Florida Gator logo. A man laden with a cooler and what looks like camera equipment trails behind him. A young woman carrying a backpack rounds out the group.

Phoebe's breath hitches in excitement, and Victor looks ready to pass out, he's so giddy. "Dr. Drake!" Victor waves. "Over here!"

Professor Drake waves back. "Ahoy!" He and his entourage make their way toward us.

Phoebe rushes forward to introduce herself. "Phoebe Van Cleave," she says meaningfully, reaching for Professor Drake's hand. "I'm the president of the Sunshine Ghost Society. We didn't get a chance to talk on the phone, but I've been looking forward to this for ages."

"Pleased to meet you, Phoebe." He shakes her hand, then dismisses her to greet the rest of our group, leaving Phoebe looking like a kid who didn't get the toy she wanted Christmas morning. I'm not sure what she expected. Just because she's the head ghoul chaser doesn't mean Mortimer Drake is supposed to fall at her feet.

The young woman is Dr. Drake's assistant, Amber Stiles. Pale, with mousy brown hair and blue eyes, she looks overwhelmed by all the introductions.

The man is the photojournalist who'll be recording our trip. Late twenties, tall, with close-cropped dark hair. Funny, I feel like I've met him before, except his hair was longer and pulled back in a ...

"*Man Bun?*" I sputter. "I mean, *um,* Wade, right? You used to work for the Cooking Channel."

He glares at me. "Lucy McGuffin. I should have known you'd be involved in this." He glances around our little group. "Looks like the whole gang is here. The name, by the way, is *Wayne* Hopkins. Not Wade or Man Bun or anything else."

My face goes hot.

Last year, a crew from the Cooking Channel was in Whispering Bay to film a reality show called *Battle of the Beach Eats.* Wayne was the original cameraman working under the show's producer, Tara Bell, but he quit following a nasty spat with her. Not that I blame him for walking out on the job. Tara was a terrible person and a horrible boss who could never get Wayne's name right (hence my reason for giving him the Man Bun moniker).

"I thought you were going to work for the public access channel," I say.

He shrugs. "I decided to go into business for myself. Independent projects allow for more artistic expression."

In other words, independent projects pay more.

"I'm, um, sure you must have heard about Tara," I say carefully.

"That she was murdered? Yeah, I heard it was one of your muffins. Poison, right?"

Brittany pushes her way forward. "No one blames Lucy for that. She can't help it if some lunatic from another town poisoned one of her muffins." She gives Wayne a big smile. "On behalf of the Whispering Bay Chamber of Commerce, we are absolutely *thrilled* that our beautiful town will be featured in your documentary. Do you know where and when it will air?"

Documentary? No one said anything yesterday about a documentary.

Victor senses my confusion. "Sorry, Lucy, I should have mentioned that."

"I only knew about the documentary because after I left your place last night, I ran into Victor at the grocery store," Brittany says. "He was nice enough to fill me in on all the details."

No wonder Phoebe took the time to style her hair and wear a dress. I wish I'd been in on this. Obviously, I need to spend more time at the Piggly Wiggly. On the other hand, would I have really dressed any differently? Besides, my *Fear The Muffin Top* T-shirt is great promo for my café.

"Wayne has been putting together an absolutely fabulous documentary chronicling all of Dr. Drake's work," Bonnie gushes. "Today will be the highlight of the piece. Everyone in the pirate community is excited to see the final results."

Paco barks, drawing our attention back to where he thinks it belongs. Meaning him.

"And who is this good-looking little fellow?" Professor Drake bends over to pat Paco on the head. "Let me guess," he says, glancing up at Victor. "This is the ghost-whispering dog you told me about?"

"Yes, this is Paco," Victor says proudly. "I can't wait until you see him in action. If Lazy Eye Louie's remains are on that island, Paco will be able to make contact with him."

If Paco could puff out his chest, he would. I feel like I should step in here and bring everyone back down to Earth. "But it's not a given. Anything could happen."

"Well, we won't know unless we try," Professor Drake says good-naturedly. "I've only chartered the boat until five this afternoon, so there's no time to waste. Shall we get started?"

My cell phone goes off. It's Travis. "You all go ahead." I hand Paco's leash to Brittany. "I'll meet you on the boat."

I wait until the group has walked far enough away to give me some privacy. "Calling to wish me good luck?" I ask my boyfriend.

"So you're still going through with this pirate cruise?" he grumbles.

"We're just about to board."

"Then you've met Professor Drake?"

"He looks just like his picture, minus the tweed." I talk and walk at the same time, making my way toward the boat so I don't hold everyone up. "He brought along an assistant, and you'll never guess who else is here. Remember Tara Bell's cameraman? The guy with the man bun?"

"Vaguely."

"Turns out his name is Wayne Hopkins and he's been working as an independent filmmaker since that day he walked out on Tara. Small world, huh?"

"Too small. I never liked that guy. There was something always off about him."

Travis has a point. If my memory serves me right, Wayne always ordered a blueberry muffin. Not that I have anything against blueberry muffins. Especially *my* blueberry muffins, but c'mon, they're pretty boring.

Now that I'm close enough to the boat, I can see the ship's name painted in big black letters, and I can't help but laugh.

"What's so funny?" Travis asks.

"You'll never believe the name of this boat."

"Try me."

"Feeling Nauti."

He snorts. "Figures."

Brittany leans over the boat's rail, right next to the tacked-on sign that reads *FEELING NAUTI EXCURSIONS. Half and Full Day tours available.* A breeze picks up the end of her braid, creating a charming picture. "Lucy! Hurry up. Captain Kip is about to give us his welcome speech!"

"Gotta go," I say to Travis. "Everyone's waiting for me."

"Hold on," he says. "I need the coordinates for this island."

"Why? Are you planning on crashing the party?" I tease.

"I need it in case there's an emergency."

Not that I'm anticipating one, but it's actually a good idea. "As a matter of fact, Victor gave me that info yesterday." I dig the paper out of my shorts pocket again and text the coordinates to Travis. "I have no idea what those numbers mean, but I just sent it to you."

"Got it," Travis says. "Look, your cell phone service might be touch and go, so promise me the minute you get back, you'll call me."

Travis is such a worrywart. But the fact he cares makes my heart go pitter-patter. "I promise. Relax! Brittany and Will are with me. And don't forget Paco. What could go wrong?"

"I don't know, McGuffin. I have a really bad feeling about this."

"No worries. I brought plenty of sunscreen."

"A sunburn isn't what I'm worried about. You have to admit, wherever you go, trouble follows."

"If by trouble, you mean Paco and I have gotten pretty darn good at solving crime around town, then I'll take that as a compliment. Look, I already told you, Victor says that Professor Drake only rented the boat until five. You know how these charter boats work. Time is money. I guarantee you we'll be back in plenty of time for me to get ready for dinner."

"You sure? Because I'm really looking forward to tonight."

"Me too. I'm already thinking of what I'm going to order."

"And you'll call the second the boat docks?"

"You have my permission to call the Coast Guard one minute after five if you don't hear from me. Feel better now?"

"Not really. But what choice do I have? You're going to do what you want anyway."

It warms my heart that Travis knows me so well. A few months ago, Travis and I exchanged the L word. Ever since then, we finish every conversation with some variation of 'I love you.' I'm about to say it when Will comes to the railing to stand beside Brittany. "Lucy! The captain says if you're not on the boat in one minute, he's leaving without you."

I say goodbye to Travis and scurry to board the *Feeling Nauti*. There will be plenty of time tonight to tell my boyfriend that I love him.

Chapter Five

A MAN WEARING A T-shirt with the words "I'm the Boss" in red letters stands at the front of the deck like he's the King of the World. It's hard to gauge how old he is, but his weather-beaten skin reveals at least a few decades at sea.

"If you haven't figured it out by now, I'm Captain Kip Kincaid, and I want to welcome you all aboard the *Feeling Nauti.*" His gravelly voice hints at a strong addiction to cigarettes. "Before we take off, I have a few rules to go over." He pauses somberly. "Think of me as a pretty flight attendant giving you emergency instructions."

This elicits a few snickers, mainly from Wayne. He pulls out his camera. "That's great stuff. Can you start again from the beginning?"

Captain Kip points to the camera and frowns. "Is that necessary?"

"You signed the release," says Professor Drake. "It's imperative we record everything that happens today." He gives Amber a meaningful look, propelling her into action.

"Sorry, I almost forgot," she mumbles as she passes around a stack of papers. "I need the rest of you to sign a release as well. Please take one and sign your name at the bottom. This gives us permission to film you for documentary purposes."

Will quickly peruses the form. "This basically says you can use the footage any way you want."

"Yes," Professor Drake says soothingly, "but it's standard language. I'm afraid my lawyer insists on it. You can't be part of the expedition without signing the release. Isn't that right, Amber?"

She jumps like she's afraid of her own shadow. "What? Oh, yes, the release. They have to be signed."

Phoebe, Victor, and Bonnie sign without question. Brittany takes a minute to read it before signing, prompting Will to grudgingly go along. I sign my release and hand it to Amber, who places it inside a folder with the rest of the papers.

"Can I continue now?" Captain Kip asks impatiently. Wayne keeps the camera pointed at him. "I'll take that as a yes," he mutters. "As I was saying, on behalf of myself and my first mate, Gary, welcome aboard the *Feeling Nauti!*"

He proceeds to take us through what sounds like a well-rehearsed series of safety instructions when his gaze meets Paco and he stops cold. Captain Kip looks at Paco like he's a worm he'd like to put on a hook. "No one said anything about a dog."

Victor steps forward to intercede. "This isn't just any dog. This is Paco. He's a very talented medium. He's going to help us talk to Lazy Eye Louie's spirit."

Captain Kip's gray mustache twitches. "You're the customer. But whoever's in charge of that *dog,* make sure you clean up after him."

Paco looks both confused and indignant. He's so used to everyone finding him charming that the idea someone might not love dogs is foreign to him.

I raise my hand. "That would be me, Lucy McGuffin. The dog won't be a problem. I have a life jacket for him and everything."

"Fine," Captain Kip concedes like we've already spent too much time on this. Before he can continue his safety talk, Phoebe interrupts to ask where the bathroom is.

"The head is below in the cabin. First door to the left. Don't anyone hog it up and we won't get into a situation."

Brittany and I exchange a look. I can only imagine the type of "situation" Captain Kip is referring to. Note taken: Use the bathroom as little as possible.

"As I was saying, I've been skippering for almost thirty years now," he says, "and I've never had an incident at sea. That's because my passengers always come first."

The hair on the back of my neck tickles. I've just caught Captain Kip in a lie. Considering that he was boasting about his safety record, I'm not exactly reassured here.

"I've only got three rules," he continues. "Rule number one: Life jackets remain on at all times while we're at sea. That includes the dog. Rule number two: If I tell you to do something, then do it."

We wait for him to continue, but he pauses long enough that Will asks, "What's rule number three?"

"Rule number three: If you throw up, you get tossed overboard."

For a second, no one says anything, then he chuckles. "Got ya!" Phoebe laughs nervously. "Seriously though, gettin' sick on board the ship can be contagious, if you know what I mean. So if you're gonna do that, do it where no one can see you. Capisce?" He walks off without waiting to see if anyone has any more questions.

A tall, thin, middle-aged man who introduces himself as Gary Olsen, the first mate, hands out life jackets. Like Captain Kip, he's wearing a T-shirt and shorts with sturdy-looking sneakers, but his attitude is much friendlier. He gives Paco a thumbs-up. "Hey, little dude. I heard you've already got your own life jacket."

Paco barks back in greeting.

"I promise, he won't be a nuisance. I'm Lucy, by the way. And this is Paco."

"Nice to meet you, Lucy." Gary grins knowingly. "Don't mind Captain Kip. It's nothing personal against Paco. He doesn't like any dog. Off or on the boat."

I thought Captain Kip's aversion to Paco was because he didn't want animals on his boat, but what kind of monster doesn't like dogs?

Someone who would lie about their safety record, that's who.

Captain Kip? Ha! More like Captain Bligh.

"Last chance to take the seasick pills," I tell Paco sternly. "You don't want to give that maniac Captain Kip the pleasure of throwing you into the gulf, do you?"

Paco growls, sounding suspiciously like a pirate. *I'd like to see him try.*

Now that the captain has had his say, Professor Drake addresses the group. "Thank you for being part of this exciting expedition! For those of you who aren't familiar with my work, I've made it my life's mission to prove the existence of the legendary José Gaspar."

He holds up a sheet of paper. "I've taken the liberty of copying a few excerpts from the diary of Luis Sánchez, the newfound link to what I believe will provide concrete proof of Gaspar's existence. Indulge me a moment while I read Sánchez's words. They've been translated for me from the original Spanish. I think once you hear this, you'll be as excited as I am."

Dr. Drake pulls a pair of eyeglasses from his shirt pocket, adjusts them over his nose and begins to read: *"The 15th of May, in the year 1795. Havana, Cuba. Today, I received a letter from my beloved mother with the crushing news that my beautiful Consuelo has married my cousin Arturo. Agony and despair course through my body. I fear that*

I may do something that will place my soul in eternal peril. How can Consuelo do this to me? For these past ten years that we have been betrothed, I have thought of nothing but her. Everything I have done was to secure our future. Alas, it has all been in vain."

Brittany gasps. "His fiancée married his *cousin?*"

Phoebe clutches my arm. "This is so sad."

Wonder of wonders. Phoebe Van Cleave actually has a heart.

Brittany and Phoebe's reaction to Luis Sánchez's diary entry makes me feel a bit coldhearted. I mean, sure, losing your fiancée to your cousin had to have stung. But engaged for *ten* years? C'mon! No one could have been expected to wait that long. Plus, there was that lazy eye of his.

"I can't believe Consuelo didn't have the guts to write him herself," says Brittany. "Can you imagine hearing from your mother that your fiancée has run off with another man?"

"Looks like Consuelo ghosted him," Will says. "Eighteenth-century style."

Dr. Drake nods sadly. "Is it any wonder that the man went AWOL? According to his diary, the next day he stole a small boat and headed for Florida. He became a bootlegger, selling liquor to disreputable establishments and notorious types."

"Like José Gaspar," says Victor.

"Exactly." Dr. Drake resumes reading. *"August 20, in the year 1796. Today I met with a most interesting fellow. At first, he refused to give his name, but after imbibing of a particularly potent ale which had the expected effect of loosening his tongue, he told me his name was Jean Marquette and that he was a member of the notorious pirate Gaspar's crew. He is entrusted to find someone to provide Gaspar's crew with liquor, and he thinks I might be the man. He is, of course, correct."*

Bonnie sucks in a breath. "Oh my. How exciting!"

Wayne slowly pans his camera around the group to get our reactions, which, for the most part, verge on awe. Bonnie is right. This is pretty cool stuff.

"After this," says the professor, "there are several more entries in which Sánchez details his business dealings with Marquette. But what I'm about to read next is the entry that's of particular interest to our cause."

"Well, don't keep us waiting," Captain Kip grumbles. "Go ahead and read it." We turn around to find him hanging back by the cabin door, listening in. Even the rough and tough Captain Kip finds this pirate stuff intriguing.

Professor Drake smiles knowingly. *"October 2, 1796,"* he reads in a smooth hypnotic tone. *"After I delivered several barrels of a most excellent ale, Gaspar is refusing to pay me what he owes. He is a shifty fellow and quite full of himself. He's right in that I can't go to the authorities and accuse him of stealing from me, but he's mistaken if he thinks I will lie down like a lamb while the wolf feasts on my carcass. Tonight, I plan to not only take what he owes me, but I am going to relieve that dog Gaspar of all his ill-gotten gold. By the time he realizes what has happened, I will be far away in New Orleans, where I will change my name and use the money to start a new life."*

"That's quite a plan," Brittany says, admiration in her voice.

"What happened?" Victor asks eagerly. "Did he steal Gaspar's gold?"

Professor Drake hands the paper to Amber, who carefully puts it away in a folder. "That was the last entry in his diary. Since we know Lazy Eye Louie absconded with pirate gold and was never heard from again, we can assume his plan worked. At least, the first part. As for the rest of it, who knows? There are two possible scenarios. He managed to escape to New Orleans and lived the rest of his life in comfortable obscurity. Or his boat crashed en route and he never made it."

Everyone starts talking at once.

"Hopefully," Dr. Drake says, quieting down the group, "we'll have an answer to that question soon. Now I want to thank all of you for being here to share in what could be the biggest day of my professional life." Once again, he looks at Amber like he's expecting her to do something. When nothing happens, he raises a brow at her, silently urging her on.

"Oh! Sorry." She dashes to a cooler and opens it to produce several bottles of champagne and a stack of plastic glasses.

Dr. Drake takes a bottle and makes a grand show of uncorking it, spilling champagne all over the deck. Paco runs to lick it up, causing Dr. Drake to laugh. "Good thing there's more where that came from." He opens a second bottle and pours champagne into the cups, filling them to the brim. Amber passes them around.

Dr. Drake raises his cup in the air and makes a toast. "To a successful expedition! If Lazy Eye Louie's remains are on this island, by golly, we'll find them. I'll *never* give up. No matter how long it takes! Long live the legend of José Gaspar!"

Everyone responds with a cheer. Not only is the champagne nice and cold, it tastes expensively yummy.

Wayne turns off his camera. "Great stuff, Professor."

Captain Kip announces it will take about an hour and a half to get to the island, and the group disperses to settle themselves for the long boat ride.

Phoebe sidles up to me. "I heard someone say you had seasick pills?"

I study Phoebe's face. She looks paler than usual, and we haven't even taken off yet. "I have Dramamine. You want some?"

She thinks about it. "I've never taken any before. What are the side effects?"

"Just some drowsiness. But it's better than the alternative."

She bites her bottom lip. "True."

I reach into my tote for the bottle and hand her a couple of the pills. She barely thanks me before taking off in search of water while Amber goes around refilling glasses with the last of the champagne.

I drain the rest of my bubbly, then pull out Paco's doggie life jacket from my tote. He's only used it once, when we went to the beach and I was afraid he'd get carried away by a current. Turned out my big bad ghost-whispering dog is afraid of sand crabs, so he didn't go anywhere near the water.

"Are you sure you don't want the seasick pill?" I ask, pulling the life jacket over his neck and securing it snugly around his chest.

Nope.

Ugh. Why is my dog so stubborn?

"Okay, but if you get sick, don't blame me."

Chapter Six

So much for having a cast-iron stomach.

I lean over the ship's rail, hoping to heck I don't lose my muffins. You'd think Captain Kip was getting a bonus to get us to the island as fast as possible.

I take a gulp of fresh sea air and count to five. There. That's a bit ... better. Paco nudges me with his nose. *You okay?* He seems genuinely concerned, which is good because I don't think I could handle any snark right now. Especially from him.

Channeling the power of positive affirmation, I try for a smile. "I'm not going to throw up, if that's what you're asking." He looks up at me with worried eyes. "Really. I'm okay."

Brittany dashes over. "Lucy, you won't believe what Wayne just told me!"

"What?" I manage to squeak out.

She blinks. "What's wrong? You sound ... oh no. Please don't tell me you're going to get sick."

"Okay, I won't, but I can't promise not to actually *get* sick." I take another gulp of air. "What did Wayne tell you?"

She looks reluctant to share now. "It can wait. You want me to get you some water?"

Just the thought of drinking anything makes it all worse. The champagne sitting in my stomach threatens to make a return trip. "What I need is some of my Dramamine." I glance around the boat looking for my tote bag. I could have sworn it was right here next to my feet. I wave her on. "Please, just tell me about Wayne. It'll help me get my mind off my stomach."

"Okay," she says, her voice hitching in excitement. "He has a meeting next week with some bigwigs from Netflix. Can you believe it? They're going to buy the pirate documentary!"

"Netflix? Brittany, what are you smoking?"

She frowns. "What do you mean?"

"You can't actually believe Netflix wants to buy a documentary from Wayne."

"What's wrong with Wayne?"

"Nothing, except he's basically a nobody. He went from the Cooking Channel to public access TV to working for himself. What kind of credentials does he have?"

The sparkle fades from her eyes. "You don't think it's legit?"

"I guess maybe it could be for real."

She nods, but her enthusiasm is watered down now. "Maybe it is too good to be true, but just think, Lucy, if we can talk to Lazy Eye Louie's ghost and get it all on film, we can finally put Whispering Bay on the map."

"It's that important to you?"

"Yes. Especially considering how I mucked up that whole *Battle of the Beach Eats* reality program."

"That was ages ago. And you can't help it if Tara was murdered and they canceled the show."

"True. You'd think Tara would have had the decency to get murdered somewhere besides Whispering Bay. After all that's happened in the past year, technically we can't call ourselves the *Safest City in America* anymore," she says, referring to the tagline she originated. "Not that it's your fault," she rushes to add, "but the executives at the Cooking Channel swear they're never coming back to town. That's why this pirate documentary is so important."

"Are you always thinking of ways to bring new business to town?"

"It's my job, Lucy."

"And you're great at it."

"Thanks. I always try my best." Her gaze flits toward the other side of the boat, where Will and Professor Drake appear deep in conversation.

"Does that include Will?" I ask softly.

She flushes. "I was hoping this trip might bring us together, but he seems determined to avoid me at all costs." She narrows her eyes thoughtfully. "I think Will is keeping a secret."

I clear my throat. "What makes you say that?"

"You're not the only one with Spidey sense. Sure, I'm not some superhuman lie detector like you are, but I can tell when a man is interested, and he was definitely interested. Then we went out on a date, and poof! *Nothing.* It's like he doesn't want me to get too close to him."

I'm dying to tell Brittany that she's right, but Will's secret isn't mine to reveal.

As if he knows we're talking about him, Will breaks away from Professor Drake to come over to our side of the boat. "What are you two up to?"

"Brittany is trying to distract me from getting sick."

"Oh." Will goes still. "Uh, is there anything I can do?"

"Besides run away, you mean?" I halfway tease.

He makes a face. "I don't do great with that kind of stuff. Did you take some Dramamine?"

"No. Do you think it's worth taking now?" I sneak a peek at Paco, who's looking rather smug. *Looks like you're the one who should have taken the pills.*

I knew he couldn't resist saying he told me so.

"Captain Kip said it'll take at least an hour and a half to get to the island, and we've only been on the water for fifteen minutes. So yeah, I'd say it's worth taking." Will glances around the deck. "Where's your bag?"

"I have no idea. I thought it was right here, but ..." Another wave of nausea crashes over me. I clutch the side rail.

"I'll go find it," Will says, scurrying off. A couple of minutes later, he comes back with a cold can of ginger ale and my tote bag.

"Where was Lucy's tote?" Brittany asks him.

"On the bench inside the cabin."

"That's weird," I say. "I could have sworn I had it with me the whole time."

Will opens the top of my tote and looks inside. "It's like Mary Poppins's carpetbag in here. There are enough supplies to last through a weekend camping trip."

"Those are all necessities. Quick. Just give me the pills."

"I don't see them." He hands my tote to Brittany. "Here, you look."

I swallow hard. "Can you guys hurry it up, please?"

Brittany rummages through the bag in frustration. "Are you sure you put the bottle back in here? There's no chance you accidentally left it on the dock, is there?"

"*What?* Yes, I'm positive I put it back. I even gave Phoebe some pills right before we took off."

"Maybe the bottle fell out of the bag," she says.

"I distinctively remember tucking the bottle back inside. At least, I think I did." I slap my hand over my mouth. "Oh no ..." I mumble through my fingers. "I think I'm gonna—"

"Please don't," Will pleads. "Brittany, why don't you take Lucy inside the cabin to lie down? I'll go look for the pills."

Brittany gently takes me by the elbow. "Okay, but hurry," she says to Will. "Things aren't looking great, if you know what I mean."

She helps me settle down onto a cushioned seat, opens up the can of ginger ale and hands it to me. Paco nudges the can, urging me on. I take a tentative sip. "Thank you," I moan.

"No worries," Brittany says. "I got your back."

"Aren't you just the teeniest bit seasick?" I ask Brittany.

"Nope. I feel great."

The sounds of happy people giddy with anticipation float around me, and I can't help but think, why am I the special one?

Even Phoebe, who thought she was getting sick earlier, looks pretty darn spry. "I heard you were down here puking," she says to me. "Thought I'd see if there was anything I could do to help."

"The only thing I need right now is Dramamine," I mutter.

She tsks. "Looks like someone should have taken their own medicine."

"Um, maybe what Lucy needs right now is some rest," Brittany says diplomatically.

"Sure. But if you need me, just yell." Phoebe shakes her head at me one last time before she leaves to join the rest of the group.

"Thanks for getting rid of her," I say. "Are you *sure* the medicine wasn't in my bag?"

"I'm positive. Will and I both looked. The bottle had to have fallen out."

Gary emerges out of the galley kitchen. "Heard you got the pukes." He hands me a small medicine cup containing two pills. "This'll help."

Brittany peers inside the cup and frowns. "Remember, Lucy, you've had a glass of champagne. Maybe you should just take one of these. Drugs and alcohol aren't the best combination."

It was actually two glasses of champagne, and right now drugs and alcohol sound like the best combination possible. I snatch the cup from Gary's hand, down the pills, then follow it with a swoosh of soda. "What was that anyway?"

Gary looks amused by my rashness. "It's Dramamine. Captain Kip keeps a bottle in his quarters. You're lucky. You got the last two pills."

Yeah, lucky me.

Paco starts to squirm. "Do you mind if I take Paco back on deck?" Brittany asks. "I think he wants to stretch his legs and get a look at the gulf."

Paco wags his tail. *Yes. Love the water.*

Ugh. Rub it in, why don't you? I wave them away. "By all means. I'll stay down here if you don't mind." Brittany and Paco take off to explore the boat, leaving me alone with Gary.

"Thank you. You've been really nice."

He smiles sympathetically. "It happens. The water is pretty choppy today."

"Does it ever happen to you? Getting seasick, I mean?"

"I've been on boats since I could crawl, so I'm used to it."

"Have you been with Captain Kip long?

"We're going on near ten years together. Before that, I was with another tourist boat, and before that, the Merchant Marines."

"Wow. You do love the water."

"My ex-wife used to say one day I'd grow gills." He pauses like he's hesitant to bother me. "I couldn't help but overhear Dr. Drake reading those diary entries. Is that stuff for real?"

"That's what we're going to find out." I sit up and take a deep breath.

"I should probably leave you alone," he says.

"No, no. It's okay. Talking actually keeps my mind off my stomach."

"Most groups rent out the boat to go deep-sea fishing or take a day trip to one of the bigger islands. This pirate thing is a first for us."

"For me too." At the curious look on his face, I go on to explain how I got here.

"The *dog* is going to be part of a séance to talk to this dead pirate named Lazy Eye Louie?" Gary asks incredulously.

"I know. Hard to believe. Look him up on Facebook. He's got his own page and everything. Only his name was Cornelius then. He's got a huge following." I take another swig of the ginger ale.

"Facebook, huh?" He chuckles. "Feeling better?"

"A little," I lie, only because he's been so nice getting me the soda and the pills and I don't want him to think it was all for nothing.

"So finding this Lazy Eye Louie would be a big deal for Dr. Drake, huh?"

"It would be huge. And not just for Dr. Drake and his career. There will be a ton of interest from the whole historical community. Who knows? Maybe the documentary Wayne is shooting might even make it to the big streaming services."

"Streaming services? You mean, like on TV?"

"It's just a rumor, but if it's true, it would be great publicity for you and Captain Kip. I bet the *Feeling Nauti* would be booked nonstop."

Gary looks taken aback. "You think so?"

Darn that champagne. I've probably said too much. I'd hate to get his hopes up based on hype being spread by Wayne, of all people. "On the other hand, this is probably all just a wild goose chase and the only thing we'll find on the island is palm trees."

The pills are starting to help. At least, I think they are. My stomach feels more settled, and I'm having a hard time keeping my eyes open. It also doesn't help that I've been up since four in the morning. Add in the potential drowsiness caused by the Dramamine coupled by the champagne I guzzled down, and it's a miracle I haven't fallen asleep already.

The sound of someone coming into the cabin forces me to shake my head clear. It's Bonnie. She sits next to me and takes my hand in hers. "How are you feeling? Brittany told me you were down here resting."

"I'm feeling better, thanks."

"Good!" She gives my hand a squeeze.

I glance around, looking for my dog.

"If you're looking for Paco, he's up on deck with Brittany. Don't worry. She's taking good care of him. He's such a smart little thing! I can't wait to see him in action."

"Have you ever worked with an animal before? You know, in this kind of situation?"

"Conjuring up a spirit? Well, I could lie to you and tell you that I have."

Uh, no you couldn't.

"I take it that would be a no, then?" I say.

Bonnie leans in closer. "Lucy, can I tell you a secret?"

Any drowsiness I was feeling earlier vanishes. A secret? I *live* for secrets. "Sure, you can tell me anything."

She lowers her voice. "I'm not a medium. I just fudged my credentials so I could be part of the expedition."

Of all the secrets I was expecting, that wasn't it.

"Won't that be a problem? I mean, aren't you afraid of what might happen when you're exposed?"

"Not really. I've done my research on Paco. From what I can tell, he's talented enough to carry the whole show."

"I ... why are you telling me all this?"

"Because I'm going to need your help to fool the rest of the group."

I blink hard. Am I dreaming this?

"I'm sorry, I don't understand. Why would I help you fool everyone?"

"Because I'm going to give you something in exchange that's going to change your world." Her lips purse together into a sly smile before she adds, "I'm the Fussy Foodie."

I'm not quite sure how to react here. I know for a fact that Bonnie is *not* the Fussy Foodie because the real Fussy Foodie is a celebrity chef named Marcus Adams. It's a big secret, and the only reason I know it is because Will and Marcus Adams share the same New York publisher. *"You're* the Fussy Foodie?"

"I'm his assistant. Which is even better. Who do you think does all the real work? I'm the one who goes to the restaurants and orders the food and does all the preliminary taste-testing. Without me, the Fussy Foodie wouldn't exist."

"So you're the one who fell in love with the doughnuts at Heidi's Bakery?"

Bonnie's eyes glaze over, and her expression turns dreamy. "I can still taste her maple bacon doughnuts on my tongue."

Well, sure, those are pretty good if you've always wanted a coronary bypass. What Bonnie said earlier about being in town a couple of months ago makes sense now. "That's when you came into The Bistro? The same day you went to Heidi's Bakery?"

She nods. "One of the Fussy Foodie's publishing friends sent him some doughnuts from Heidi's Bakery in the hope that he'd like what he tasted. Which he did. So, Marcus ... *um* the Foodie asked me to come to Whispering Bay and scope out the place. Something about a fake blogger impersonating the Foodie and a murder? Sounds a bit fantastical to me," she says, rolling her eyes, "but I do what I'm told. So I hopped on a plane and flew down, and while I was here I popped into all the local restaurants for future material. Everything was very low-key."

I bite my tongue before I say anything that might expose Will as J.W. Quicksilver. It was through Will as J.W. Quicksilver that the Fussy Foodie took an interest in Whispering Bay and Heidi's Bakery. It's obvious, however, that Bonnie has no idea that Will and J.W. Quicksilver are the same person.

"You said you wanted to exchange something. What exactly are we talking about here?"

"You're going to help me fake it through the séance so that Phoebe and Victor don't catch on. Like I said, it shouldn't be a big deal. Paco is the one who does all the real work, right?"

"Well, yeah," I say carefully.

"And for helping me, the Fussy Foodie is going to give The Bistro by the Beach a five-spoon review." At the look on my face, she adds, "A totally deserved rating! What I said earlier about your muffins was the honest-to-goodness truth. As the Fussy Foodie's assistant, I've been all over the country, and I have to say, Lucy, your muffins are by far the best I've ever tasted."

I'm speechless. Not about my muffins being the best she's ever tasted. That part is a given. But the other stuff?

"You're probably wondering why I'm going to such trouble to be part of this expedition," Bonnie says.

"Now that you mention it, yes."

"It all comes down to money. As the Fussy Foodie's assistant, I pretty much do everything for him, including act as a liaison between him and his agent. Now what I'm going to tell you, Lucy, is strictly confidential, but I can trust you, right?"

I nod so hard my head might fall off.

"The Fussy Foodie is getting his own show on Netflix. The contract was just signed a few weeks ago."

I read about the Netflix deal on the internet. The entire culinary world is waiting with bated breath for the big reveal that will expose the Fussy Foodie's true identity. It's a brilliant marketing scheme. "I don't think the Netflix deal is a secret."

"No, but this next part is." She pauses dramatically. "I'm leaving the Fussy Foodie and venturing out to produce independent projects to sell to streaming companies like Netflix. There's a huge demand for content, and after all these years working for the Foodie, I've made enough contacts that I can swing this. I have two investors already waiting in the wings." Her face darkens. "I earn peanuts as the Foodie's assistant, but as a producer of high-quality documentary films? This is the break I've been waiting for."

Wayne's claim that Netflix was interested in his pirate documentary doesn't seem so ludicrous anymore. "So you're going to produce Dr. Drake's documentary? For Netflix?"

"Or HBO or whoever bids the highest," she says.

Holy wow. This is *big*.

"And Dr. Drake is on board with this?" I ask her.

"He's been a bit resistant to the idea, but that's only because he hasn't met me in person." She flushes. "Bonnie Clark isn't my real name. It's Bonnie Albritton. I didn't want to take a chance that Dr. Drake would recognize my name from my emails and shoot me down before I'd had a chance to talk to him. Once I get a real opportunity to sell him on the idea, there's absolutely no way he can refuse. The money he'll get from the deal will fund his research for the next decade."

"Tell me more," I urge. "How did all this happen?"

"While I was fielding calls for Marcus—er, the Fussy Foodie, I met Wayne. He was trying to get some camera work, but unfortunately, we couldn't hire him—union details and all that—but he told me about this pirate documentary he was working on with Dr. Mortimer Drake. I'd been thinking about leaving the Foodie for a long time, but I've been waiting for the right opportunity. And this is it. If I can get Dr. Drake to listen to me, I know I can get him on board."

"How did you manage to fool Phoebe and Victor into thinking you were a medium?"

"Wayne helped with that. He told Professor Drake he'd worked with me before on another project and recommended me for the expedition."

I let it all sink in. Bonnie has gone to a lot of trouble to get to Professor Drake. On the other hand, if she can go from an underappreciated flunky to producing documentary films, it will be worth all the subterfuge. As a businesswoman, I can't help but admire her pluck.

"So, what do you say, Lucy? Will you help me?"

A five-spoon review from the Fussy Foodie? I'd be a fool to turn down her offer. I can't wait until Heidi finds out. "Absolutely."

Bonnie beams at me. "Fantastic!"

Chapter Seven

I WAKE UP FEELING like my mouth is stuffed with cotton. "Where am I?" I glance around. Oh. Right. I'm on the boat ride from hell.

"You're not going to throw up, are you?" Will peers down at my face in both concern and horror. Men are such wimps.

"Relax. I'm okay." I take a sip of the ginger ale. It's flat. And alarmingly warm. "What time is it?"

"Almost ten. We landed about thirty minutes ago. Professor Drake insisted they start the expedition immediately. Everyone is on the island except Gary. He's going to stay behind to man the boat."

"Captain Kip went on the expedition? I got the impression he thinks this is all a bunch of bunk."

Will shrugs. "Maybe he wants to be in the documentary?"

Speaking of the documentary ... "Will, you're never going to believe this. Bonnie Clark isn't really a medium. Her name is Bonnie Albritton, and she's the Fussy Foodie's assistant!" I fill Will in on everything Bonnie told me, including her offer to write up a five-spoon review for The Bistro in exchange for my help during the séance.

Will looks skeptical. "She's working behind the scenes with Wayne?"

"It looks that way. What do you think? She didn't lie to me, but does her story make sense to you? She let it slip that the Fussy Foodie's real name is Marcus. Oh, and don't worry. I'm pretty sure she has no clue that you're J.W. Quicksilver."

He scratches the stubble on his chin. "I've never met the Fussy Foodie's assistant, but her story pans out."

"Isn't it exciting? The Bistro by the Beach is going to get a five-spoon review from the Fussy Foodie!"

"The Fussy Foodie's assistant, you mean." He gives me a look. "Maybe Bonnie will come through, but anything can happen. You know the old saying: Don't count your chickens before they're hatched."

"I would think a big award-winning author like you could come up with a better cliché than that."

"I just don't want you to get disappointed, that's all."

"When I woke up this morning, I had no chance of a five-spoon review from the Fussy Foodie, and now I do. How can I be disappointed?" I scan the cabin for signs of my dog. "Is Paco on the island too?"

"Yeah, but no worries, Brittany is looking out for him."

How are Brittany and Will supposed to fall madly in love if she's out on the island and he's here with me? I stand up. Luckily, I'm not dizzy. And best of all, the horrible seasickness is gone.

"I'm surprised you're the one who volunteered to babysit me. You looked pretty green around the gills yourself just thinking I might throw up."

Will's expression turns sheepish. "Brittany insisted on staying with you so I could go on the expedition, but I felt kind of crummy the way I acted earlier. So we played rock paper scissors to see who would take care of you."

"Did the winner go on the island or stay on the boat?"

"I'll take that secret to my grave, thanks." He grins, and we both end up laughing. *This* is a prime example of why Brittany and Will belong together. Will was really looking forward to this pirate expedition, yet he still cared enough to stay behind and take care of me. Same with Brittany. It would be hard to find two more loyal friends.

Gary pops down into the cabin, his face scrunched with worry. "You feeling better?" Considering he just met me, it's awful sweet of him to be so concerned.

"Much better, thank you."

He nods, relieved. "You'll probably want to join the others as soon as possible. I listened to the itinerary Professor Drake has planned. An entire day of island exploring, a potential séance, and a top-rate picnic lunch. You really don't want to miss it."

"I thought we'd come back here to eat lunch," Will says.

"On a beautiful day like this?" Gary laughs nervously. "No! When we do day excursions, we always provide an on-site meal for our guests. Captain Kip and Wayne took the provisions with them. No need for the guests to do anything. The captain will set everything up."

The hair on the back of my neck tingles. Gary has just lied to me. But about what? This is the most frustrating thing about my "gift." I can tell when someone is lying, but I can't tell exactly what they're lying about. The way I figure it, there were at least four things in his statement that could be a lie.

1. They always provide lunch for their guests.

2. The lunch is "top-rate."

3. Captain Kip and Wayne took the provisions with them.

4. Gary's reassurance that there will be no need for any of the

guests to do anything because Captain Kip will set it all up.

Since Captain Kip Kinkaid strikes me as more of the "here's your lunch and don't bother me" type, I highly suspect number 4 is the lie. Oh, and number 2. I have no idea what Gary's idea of a "top-rate" lunch is, but I'm pretty sure that as the Fussy Foodie's assistant, Bonnie will be sorely disappointed.

I grab my tote and nudge Will out of the cabin, where I'm hit by a blast of bright Florida sunshine. The forecast called for cloudy skies with a slight chance of rain later this evening, but it looks as if Mother Nature has her own agenda, which is fine by me. I'll take blue skies and sunshine every day of the week.

My first impression of the island is that it's big, with lots of shrubs and palm trees. I don't see anyone, which means Paco and the rest of the gang are buried somewhere inside all that dense foliage.

I kick off my sneakers. "How on earth has no one explored this island before?" I ask, going down the boat's ladder. "It's huge." Landing in knee-deep water, I slosh my way to shore.

"Beats me," Will says, following behind. "But looks can be deceiving. Just because we can't see the other end of the island doesn't mean that it's big."

Once I'm on solid land, I consider keeping my sneakers off, but the last thing I need is to step on some exotic island bug and get bit. With my luck, the bite will fester into an infection, and I'll get gangrene. No, thank you.

"Which direction do you think they went?"

Will points to a flurry of footprints marring the otherwise smooth sand. "I say we follow the trail."

"Good idea." I pull a bottle of water from my tote, and lo and behold, the missing bottle of Dramamine falls onto the sand. Even though the air is warm, goosebumps break out over my arms.

"I could have sworn the Dramamine wasn't in your bag." Will scoops up the bottle and looks inside my tote. "You've got so much stuff in there, we must have overlooked it. What is that? Muffins?" He pulls out a large zip-lock bag and takes out an apple walnut cream cheese muffin. It's my specialty muffin and Will's favorite.

I don't blame him for being distracted by my muffins, but currently I'm more interested in the bottle of Dramamine.

"You and Brittany looked through my tote and the bottle wasn't there. And now it is. Are you trying to tell me that *both* of you missed it?"

He takes a bite of muffin and chews thoughtfully. "What? You think someone took the bottle and then put it back inside your bag? Why would anyone do that?"

"I have no idea." I open the cap and peer inside the bottle, but it's impossible to tell if any of the pills are missing. "According to the label, there should be fifty tablets. Hold out your hands."

"What for?"

"Because we're going to count them."

Will makes a face like he doesn't see the point, but he snarfs down the rest of his muffin, allowing me to dump the pills into his upturned palms. He quickly counts them out. "That's forty-two pills."

"I bought this bottle a few months ago when I had an inner ear infection, but I only took one dose, so that was two pills. I should have forty-eight left."

"I saw you and Phoebe talking. Didn't you give her some pills?"

"Oh. Right. I gave her two pills. That leaves forty-six. So what happened to the other four pills?"

"Maybe you took them and forgot?"

Not likely, but that inner ear infection did have me a little loopy, so it's possible I took a couple more doses and just don't remember. But that doesn't account for how the bottle went missing and has now magically reappeared.

Will reads my mind. "Maybe someone took the bottle from your tote, then put it back later because they were too embarrassed to ask you for the medication?"

"Why would anyone be embarrassed to ask for Dramamine?"

"I don't know. Maybe it's a macho thing."

"Or maybe the bottle was in the tote all along and you and Brittany just missed it?"

"Maybe. Who knows? Who cares?"

Will's right. We have more important things to worry about than a few missing Dramamine tablets. Like catching up to Paco. I really hope he hasn't made contact with Lazy Eye Louie yet. I know Brittany will take good care of him, but I prefer to be present when my dog is communing with the dead.

I loop the tote over my shoulder, and we follow the trail of footsteps. Now that Will and I are alone, it's the perfect opportunity to bring up the Brittany situation. "Can I ask you a personal question? What's the real reason you never asked Brittany out on a date again? And you might as well tell me the truth, because if you lie, I'll know it."

He shakes his head at me. "You and that gift of yours."

"Tell me about it. Sometimes it feels more like a curse." I tell him how Captain Kip lied about his safety record.

"That's the kind of lie I would have rather not known about."

"You and me both. Being a human lie detector isn't all it's cracked up to be."

He eyes me. "Can you still not tell when Travis is lying?"

"Nope."

Ironic, isn't it? My boyfriend is the only person on the planet I can't catch in a lie. But it wasn't always like that.

When Travis first came to town, I could read him like a book (think *Pride and Prejudice,* because besides knowing whenever he lied, I also took an instant dislike to him the same way Elizabeth Bennet did with Mr. Darcy).

But just like Darcy did with Elizabeth, Travis won me over, and it became harder to figure out if he was lying or telling the truth. And now that I'm in love with him, it's like my Spidey sense has abandoned me. Travis Fontaine could tell me he's going to Mars tomorrow and I would probably believe him. Well, maybe I wouldn't be quite *that* gullible.

A while back I had the opportunity to meet Jenny, Paco's original owner. She called him Darwin, which is a perfectly lovely name, but I think Paco suits him better. Jenny was also a human lie detector—until she fell in love and got married, causing her to mysteriously lose her gift. She implied the same thing could happen to me.

So far, my relationship with Travis hasn't altered my abilities. As a matter of fact, my lie-detecting barometer is as sharp as ever. Maybe it's the marriage part that changes things up.

Just thinking about it makes my stomach go sour. All my life I've dreamed of what it would be like to be "normal." To not have to smile at someone and pretend I don't know they've just lied to my face or hurt my feelings.

But lately, I've begun to look at my special skills as a true gift. If I get married and lose my ability to sniff out a lie, will I also lose my ability to communicate with Paco? If it happened to Jenny, it could happen to me too.

Will waves a hand in front of my face. "Earth to Lucy."

"Sorry. I was just thinking." I glance around to find us closed in by tropical brush. The scenery looks the same as it did a few minutes ago. "Are you sure we're heading in the right direction? I feel like we're going around in circles."

"The footprints aren't so visible here," he admits. "But they had to have gone this way." He looks at me sideways. "What's got you so distracted? You looked like you were on another planet."

"I was just thinking about Travis."

"Seems like the two of you are pretty tight."

"We are." I take a deep breath. "As a matter of fact, I think he's the one."

Will's expression softens. "I'm happy for you, Lucy."

"Really?"

"Of course. You're my best friend."

"If I'm really your best friend, then you'll answer my earlier question. Why didn't you ask Brittany out on a second date? And don't tell me it's because you don't like her, because I know you do."

I'm expecting him to dodge my question again when he surprises me with a long-suffering sigh. "I can't start a relationship with anyone unless I tell them that I'm J.W. Quicksilver."

"Is that all? You make it sound as if telling people that you're this famous author is the end of the world."

"It would be the end my world."

"Don't you think you're being a tad melodramatic?"

"Do you know how much pressure my publishing company is putting on me to go on a book tour? And it's not just a US tour. They want me to go Scotland and Australia and—"

"Oh, boo-hoo. You poor world-famous author you. Forced to travel around the world so your fans can shower you with adulation."

"I'm serious, Lucy."

Will's somber tone makes me stop in my tracks.

"Think about it. Once everyone knows that I'm J.W. Quicksilver, they'll expect me to quit my job and write full-time. My agent texts me at least twice a day wondering what the heck I'm doing working as a librarian in a little nowhere town."

"Hey! On behalf of the residents of Whispering Bay, I take exception to that description."

He shrugs miserably.

It never occurred to me that Will might have to leave his job if everyone knew he was J.W. Quicksilver. "No one could force you to quit."

"No, but everything would change. You know it would," he adds meaningfully. "I don't know. Lately I've been thinking it might be a good idea to quit the library. I don't need the money, that's for sure."

If Will quit his job at the Whispering Bay Public Library, he wouldn't have a reason to come into The Bistro every morning and get a cup of coffee on his way to work. And if he was on a world tour, he wouldn't be around to get pizza and watch *America's Most Vicious Criminals* every Friday night. It wouldn't just be his life that would change. Mine would too.

Maybe Will has a point. Maybe things are perfect the way they are. At least, that's what the selfish part of me thinks. But is that being fair to Will? Or Brittany?

"Sooner or later, the world will find out that I'm Quicksilver. I just want to do it on my own terms, you know?" He glances around. "I think you're right. I think we're going around in circles."

"Maybe we should call out." I cup my hands around my mouth. "Yoo-hoo! Where is everyone? Paco! Can anyone hear me?"

Instead of a human voice, a shrill coo answers back. Having lived in Florida all my life, I'm used to all sorts of bugs and insects, but I've never heard anything like this before. "What was that?"

"Probably the usual tropical island creature," Will says.

"Such as?"

His blue eyes twinkle with mischief. "Lions and tigers and bears."

I'm sure Will thinks he's being funny, but all I can think about is Paco. Knowing he's with Brittany reassures me somewhat, but my little dog can be stubborn. What if he decides to chase down some exotic island creature and gets bit? On the other hand, he is afraid of sand crabs, so maybe I have nothing to worry about.

"Lucy, the correct response to lions and tigers and bears is, 'oh my.'"

"Ha ha. Why haven't we run into anyone? You'd think Paco would have heard me calling and come running."

"Maybe you weren't loud enough." He throws his head back and yells, "Hello! Anyone out there? Paco! Brittany! Anyone?"

There's no response.

"You're right," Will says. "I'm beginning to get a bad feeling about this."

A rustling noise in the trees causes us to whip around. Brittany emerges from a clump of greenery, looking ... well, not very Brittany-like, that's for sure. She's missing the adorable sailor hat, and her French braid looks a mess. Even her white pants are smudged with dirt. But more alarmingly, she's alone.

She smashes me into a hug. "Oh, thank God! I heard you shouting, so I came running."

"Where's Paco? Is he with Victor or Phoebe?"

"He ran away." Her voice is wobbly with tears. "I'm sorry, Lucy, but I can't find him anywhere."

Chapter Eight

I SWALLOW DOWN MY dread and focus on the fact that while she looks shaken, Brittany seems physically unharmed.

Will places his hand on her shoulder. "Are you all right? What happened?"

I take a bottle of water from my tote and offer it to her. Brittany takes a large gulp before saying, "After we got off the boat, Professor Drake suggested we break up into small groups. That way we could cover more ground in less time."

"Makes sense," Will says.

"Paco and I teamed up with Victor. Everything was fine, and then suddenly, Paco took off."

"Maybe he connected with Lazy Eye Louie's spirit," Will says.

Brittany avoids my gaze. "Yeah, hopefully. That would be great, wouldn't it?"

Brittany is such a terrible liar that even Will catches on. He and Brittany exchange a look reminiscent of the one they shared last night when Will was scrolling through websites and he lied to me about what they were reading.

There's only one thing the two of them would want to hide from me ...

I take a deep breath. "All right. I'll say it out loud. Did Paco chase a squirrel? Is that how he got lost?"

"Squirrel?" Brittany blinks hard. "Here? On this island?"

"Brittany, you can't honestly think you can lie to me and get away with it."

Her shoulders crumble. "I'm sorry, Lucy. I knew the Mexican tree squirrels here were gigantic, but I had no idea they could fly. I mean, the article *did* mention they could fly, but—"

"Fly?" I shriek. "As in, swooping down from the sky kind of flying?"

"No, silly. They're not birds. They fly tree-to-tree. It's probably more of a hopping motion."

Will groans. "Brittany, I think you better stop while you're ahead."

I narrow my eyes at him. "You knew about these flying squirrels, didn't you? *That's* what the two of you were looking at on your phone last night. You knew there were giant killer squirrels on this island, and you didn't say anything." I don't know whether to be hurt or angry. Or terrified. I think I'm all three.

"I'm sorry," Brittany says. "We didn't try to hide it from you. Not exactly."

Will looks up into the trees. "I honestly didn't think we'd run into them. The article said they were native to some of the islands here on the Gulf of Mexico, but what are the odds?"

"So you were willing to play Russian roulette with my dog's life!"

Will has the decency to look ashamed. "Look, I get it. Everyone has an Achilles' heel. Squirrels are yours, and we should have told you about them. But Lucy, there's no such thing as a killer squirrel. They're just harmless little rodents."

"With adorably fluffy tails," Brittany says, then seeing my expression, hastily adds, "Lucy is right. They can be terrible pests. But Will is right, too. I've never heard of a squirrel actually *killing* anyone."

I could argue that point, but now isn't the time. For Paco's sake, I need to get my act together.

"I know I'm irrational when it comes to squirrels, but we don't have time to debate this right now. We need to focus on Paco. Show me a picture of this Mexican tree squirrel so I know what we're up against."

Will pulls his cell phone from the back pocket of his shorts and swipes through his screen. "No internet service."

I'm not surprised, but it was worth a try.

"Okay, so what happened exactly?" I ask Brittany. "Paco saw one of these squirrels and took off running?"

"Victor and I were walking through the brush with Paco in front of us. He was doing a great job sniffing at everything, and I thought for sure he was onto something so I took him off his leash, when this squirrel came out of nowhere and Paco took off after it."

"Speaking of Victor, where is he?" Will asks.

Brittany takes another swig of the water. "We got separated chasing after Paco. I thought I saw Paco dashing through the shrubs, but then I tripped, and I haven't seen him since." Tears well in her eyes. "If anything happens to that sweet little dog, I'll never forgive myself."

"You say you broke up into groups to explore the island?" Will asks her.

Brittany nods. "Victor, Paco and I were in one group. Professor Drake, Bonnie, and Phoebe were in another group, and Wayne and Amber went off to explore on their own."

"What about Captain Kip?" Will asks.

"He went fishing. He showed us this pretty little clearing near a brook. We're supposed to rendezvous there every hour in case one of us finds something."

"I'm shocked Wayne and his camera weren't up Professor Drake's butt," I say.

Will raises a brow like he too thinks it's odd that Wayne wouldn't be in Dr. Drake's group.

"Phoebe suggested Wayne shoot some footage of the island. I'm pretty sure she was trying to get Professor Drake alone, but then Bonnie ruined her plan by inserting herself into their group."

"Why would Phoebe want to get Professor Drake alone?" I ask.

Brittany giggles. "Because she has a crush on him, silly."

"Phoebe? A crush on Professor Drake?"

"Don't act so surprised. Didn't you notice she wore lipstick today?"

"Well, yeah, but I thought—"

"Trust me, Lucy. I'm good at reading those kinds of things." Brittany's gaze lingers on Will longer than necessary, making him flush.

Could Brittany be on to something?

Phoebe Van Cleave and Professor Mortimer Drake?

Ew.

Normally, I'd take Brittany's word on this, but I've known Phoebe a long time. She's way too self-absorbed to have a crush on anyone. The only thing she seems to care about is her silly ghost society.

All this talk of crushes makes Will clear his throat. "I think our best shot at finding Paco is to retrace Brittany's steps."

"Good idea, but let's be careful not to get separated," Brittany says. "Victor is still out there somewhere. With any luck, he's found Paco."

The three of us form a single-file line with Brittany in front. Sweat drips down my forehead. It's not even noon yet and the heat is beginning to get to me. Hopefully, we'll find Paco soon. It's not like him to chase down a squirrel for this long. Maybe he's lost and trying to find his way back to us. Or maybe he's found Lazy Eye Louie's remains. It's the only thing that makes sense.

An image of my little dog, standing guard over the ghost of a long-ago dead pirate, gives me the creeps. Sure, this is what he does, but as far as I know, Paco has only communed with the recently dead. And none of those ghosts were notorious bootleggers or thieves. I really hope this Lazy Eye Louie isn't filling Paco's head with a bunch of pirate nonsense.

We get through the brush and emerge into a small clearing.

"Is this the meetup spot?" I ask Brittany.

She nods. "We're supposed to meet here at ten forty-five."

Will checks his watch. "That's ten minutes from now."

A scream cuts through the air, making me jump. "What was that?"

We whip around at the sound of pounding footsteps. Victor pushes aside a shrub and bends over to catch his breath. His hair is mussed, and his clothes are filthy.

"Victor!" Brittany says. "Where have you been?"

"Looking for you." He glances around wildly. "Did you find Paco?"

"Not yet," Brittany says.

Victor looks crestfallen. "At least you were able to find Lucy and Will." He looks at me with kind eyes. "Feeling better, Lucy?"

"Much," I say. "Thank you."

"Did you hear the scream?" Will asks Victor.

"I sure did." He jerks his head to the right. "It came from over there." He glances at Brittany. "I thought it was you. That's why I came running."

"It wasn't me, but it definitely sounded female."

"Well, if it wasn't Brittany and it wasn't me," I say, "that only leaves Amber, Bonnie, or Phoebe."

Speak of the devil. Phoebe comes out of the shrubs, looking even more disheveled than Brittany. The island humidity has done a real number on her formerly sleek bob, giving her a kind of crazed Albert Einstein look. "What's going on?" she demands like we're a bunch of her former students she's just caught skipping class.

Victor takes in Phoebe's appearance and frowns. "Phoebe, are you all right? I've never seen you look so ... um ..."

"I'm fine," she snaps. She looks between me and Brittany. "What happened? Why did you scream?"

"It wasn't me," Brittany says. "Or Lucy either. We thought it was you."

Phoebe looks down her nose at us. "Don't be ridiculous. I've never screamed in my life."

"It's true," Victor says. "Phoebe is much too dignified to scream."

"Then that leaves the undignified Amber or Bonnie." Will glances behind Phoebe. "Weren't you with Bonnie and Professor Drake? We thought the three of you went exploring together."

She sniffs. "I thought they were behind me, but they must have gotten lost in the brush."

My neck feels like it's crawling with ants. Hoo boy. I've just caught Phoebe in a lie.

Victor, who doesn't have my gift, buys her fib—hook, line and sinker. "That's what happened to me and Brittany," he says sympathetically. "This island is one big maze."

Phoebe scans the group like she's just realized a vital member of our team is missing. "Where's Paco?"

"Sadly, he's missing in action," Victor says. "Some business about chasing down a squirrel. But I'm sure the little fellow is close by. For all we know, he might have already found Lazy Eye Louie."

"Let's keep moving," Will says. "And this time, everyone stick together. No matter what."

As we trek through the brush, I can't help but wonder what's behind Phoebe's lie. Maybe it's as simple as not wanting to admit that she's the one who got lost. If anyone has too much pride, it's Phoebe Van Cleave.

"Help! Please!" A female voice jolts me out of my thoughts.

Will halts in his tracks. "Did you hear that?"

We rush ahead to find Amber kneeling over Wayne. He's stretched out on the ground, and from what I can see, he's not moving.

"Well, this doesn't look good," Brittany says.

Amber jerks her head up, her eyes frantic. "Please help him. He must have tripped and hit his head."

Wayne moans, propelling us all into action. Will helps him sit up as Wayne rubs the top of his head and winces.

"Thank God you're not dead," Amber says.

Wayne blinks, then stares her at with a glazed expression. "What happened?"

"What do you remember?" Will asks.

"Not much. One minute I was shooting some landscape, and the next thing I know I got whacked in the head."

The group exchanges a worried look. I'm pretty sure I'm not the only one who notices Wayne is slurring his words.

"Whacked in the ..." Amber looks stunned. "You think someone *hit* you?"

"Wait," I say. "Weren't the two of you together?"

"Yes, but Wayne kept rushing ahead, and in all this brush, I lost sight of him."

"She walks like a snail," Wayne grumbles. He looks around the ground. "Where's my camcorder?"

Everyone begins searching, but there's no sign of Wayne's camera. "Maybe it got tossed into the brush when you fell," Amber says.

"I didn't fall," Wayne says thickly. He smacks his lips together. "My mouth feels like the Sahara Desert."

I give him a bottle of water. He chugs it all down in one gulp.

"Maybe you tripped on something?" Victor suggests. "A tree root? Or perhaps a small bush?"

"I did *not* trip. I was knocked to the ground." Wayne's voice rises in panic. "Someone did this on purpose to steal my camera."

"That's preposterous," says Phoebe. "Who would want to steal your camera?"

"How the hell should I know?" He rubs the top of his head again. *"Damn."*

"We should probably cut this expedition short so we can get you to a doctor," Will says.

Wayne keeps searching the ground. "I don't need a doctor. What I need is my camcorder."

"Will is right," Brittany says. "You sound like you're drunk. You might have a concussion. It's best to get you checked out as soon as possible."

Victor sadly shakes his head. "I hate to say it, but I must concur. We need to find Captain Kip and get back to Whispering Bay so we can get you proper medical help."

"I agree, but we can't go anywhere until we find Paco," I say firmly.

"And Professor Drake and Bonnie," Victor adds. "Where do you think they could be?"

"Where did you last see them?" Will asks Phoebe.

"I'm not sure. Like I said, they must have gotten lost in the brush."

There go the phantom ants again, crawling up and down my neck. I wish Phoebe would stop with this ridiculous lie of hers. I'm about to confront her when I hear a whining sound.

Brittany hears it too. "Is that what I think it is?"

"Paco!" I yell.

The whimpering becomes louder.

"This way," I cry over my shoulder, running toward the sound of my dog. We arrive at a small clearing. It looks similar to the area where we're supposed to meet up for lunch, but there's no brook. Paco is sitting there, his back to me, his silhouette rigid, like's he's in the grip of a spell. A spell I've become all too familiar with this past year. "Paco!"

At the sound of my voice, he turns his head, and we lock gazes.

"You naughty dog! I was—" Something in his eyes stops me cold. Seeing my reaction, the rest of the group freezes.

"Did he find Lazy Eye Louie's remains?" Victor asks breathlessly.

I walk over to where Paco stands guard and glance down at the lifeless body crumpled in front of him.

Holy wow. I wasn't expecting *this.*

The rest of the group edges closer to get a better look.

Amber lets out another scream (she's good at those).

"It's Professor Drake," Wayne says. "And he looks ..."

"Dead," says Will.

Paco looks up at me. *Yep.*

Chapter Nine

WILL CROUCHES NEXT TO the professor's body and places his fingers on the side of his neck. "No pulse." He gently lifts the dead man's head and feels around with his hands. Blood oozes through Will's fingers. "It looks like he fell and hit his head on something." He glances around the ground. "A rock, maybe?"

No one says anything for a few long minutes. I think we're all too stunned.

Victor comes forward to examine the gash on Dr. Drake's head. "What are the odds that both the professor and Wayne fell and hit their heads on a rock?"

"How many times do I have to tell you morons I didn't fall?" Wayne snarls. "I was attacked!"

"No," Phoebe whispers in horror. "Dr. Drake *can't* be dead. He simply can't be."

Paco barks. *Professor says he didn't fall. Someone hit him from behind.*

Someone hit the professor? On purpose? I fight back a shudder. Then that would mean that the professor was *murdered.*

My brain goes a thousand places at the same time.

I need to share this information with the rest of the group, and if it was just Will and Brittany, I could, but I can't very well tell everyone else that I can read my dog's thoughts. Of course, this group does believe in ghosts and the power of seances, but still ... my only course of action is to logically steer them in the right direction.

"Victor has a point," I say. "The odds of the Professor and Wayne both tripping and hitting their heads is pretty slim."

Will walks around the area, studying the ground. A small bundle of neatly stacked palm fronds at the base of a tree catches his attention. It looks as if someone arranged them there on purpose to hide something.

Will must be thinking the same thing because he lifts a few fronds off the stack to reveal a black object. "I think we found Wayne's missing camcorder."

Wayne practically knocks Will out of the way to scoop up his camera. "Thank God!" Then he spots something on the camera, and his expression turns blank.

I spot it too. It's blood.

Paco looks at me with sad eyes. *Told you someone hit the professor.*

This is the physical evidence I need to share Paco's take on the professor's death. "It looks like someone used Wayne's camcorder to hit Professor Drake on the head."

Brittany spins around to look at me. "Lucy, are you saying Professor Drake was *murdered?*"

Amber starts crying.

The color drains from Phoebe's face. "I ... this can't be happening." She stumbles and grabs onto Victor's arm for support.

"I've got you, my dear." Victor helps her to the ground, where she settles herself into a cross-legged position. Brittany pulls a bottle of water from my tote and offers it to her. You'd think with all of Phoebe's ghostly experiences, she'd be more composed at the sight of a dead body.

"If Professor Drake was murdered," Victor says, "then that means ..." He shakes his head like he can't believe what he's about to say.

So I'll say it for him. "It means that unless there's someone else on this island, one of us is a murderer." I turn to Wayne. "It looks like your theory is right. Someone must have hit you on the head to steal your camera. Then they used it to kill Dr. Drake."

"Finally," Wayne says, "someone with a brain. This camera," he says, holding it up in the air, "is proof that I was attacked. Whoever you are, don't think I'm not going to press charges. You're going to pay for what you did to me!"

Assault seems like a minor charge compared to murder, but I'm not about to challenge Wayne. He's definitely more alert than before, but his words still sound thick.

Brittany sucks in a breath. "What do we do now?"

Amber sniffles. "I say we get off this horrible island right away."

"What about Bonnie?" Victor asks. "She's still missing."

Phoebe looks up with watery eyes. "I'd almost forgotten about Bonnie."

"The first order of business is to find Captain Kip," I say. "He can use the radio on the boat to notify the authorities about the professor. Once the police know about Professor Drake, we can get Wayne back to Whispering Bay to see a doctor so he can get his head checked out."

"I don't need a doctor," Wayne insists, fidgeting with his camera.

"I don't think you should touch that camera," Will says.

"Why not? It's mine."

"Because based on what we know so far, it's most likely the murder weapon. The authorities will want to dust it for fingerprints."

"Well since my fingerprints were already on it, it isn't going to matter, is it?" Wayne pushes a few buttons on the camera, then stills. "Damn it! All the footage I took today has been erased."

"You sure about that?" Will asks.

"I'm not an idiot." Wayne shows him the screen.

Will is careful not to touch the camera while studying it. "Wayne is right. All the footage is gone."

"How odd," says Victor.

"There's nothing *odd* about it," Wayne says. "Whoever murdered Professor Drake not only hit me on the head to steal *my* camera, they erased all my footage too." He gazes around in wild-eyed disgust. "Can't you people see what's happening? Someone's trying to frame me!"

Hoo boy, talk about paranoia.

Victor says what we're all thinking. "That makes no sense. If someone is trying to frame you, why would they hit you on the head? It makes you appear like another victim, not the perpetrator. Clearly, you haven't thought that theory through."

"Why would anyone erase the film on Wayne's camera?" Brittany asks.

"Because they're trying to sabotage my documentary, that's why." Wayne narrows his eyes at Victor. "And I dare you to tell me that theory doesn't make sense."

"No, no," Victor says. "You're correct on that point. The only logical explanation for erasing the film is that someone doesn't want the documentary made."

We all glance at one another suspiciously.

"Are you able to stand up?" Victor asks Phoebe, concern written all over his face.

She meekly hands the bottle of water back to Brittany and stands. "I'm fine."

"Let's find Captain Kip and get off this island," he says.

"What about Professor Drake?" Amber asks. "Are we just going to leave him here alone? What if animals ..." Her voice trails off, and she starts crying again.

An image of those horrible Mexican tree squirrels jumping on top of Professor Drake's lifeless body pops into my head. Thanks a lot, Amber. Nothing short of therapy is going to erase that from my brain.

"Amber has a point," Will says. "Technically, this is a crime scene. I'll stay here to make sure nothing happens to the professor's remains."

"Really?" Amber wipes away a tear. "That's so sweet of you."

"I'll stay with Will," Brittany offers.

I'm expecting Will to politely (yet firmly) decline Brittany's offer. Instead, he says, "Thanks, Brittany. I wouldn't mind some company."

I feel a responsibility to point out the obvious. "Most likely it will be the Coast Guard who responds first, but I have no idea how long it might take them to get here. The two of you could be here for hours."

Brittany eyes my bag. "Leave your tote with us. There's plenty of water and snacks in there, right?"

When I'd envisioned Will and Brittany on a deserted island, babysitting a corpse hadn't been part of the picture, but hey, I can work with this. The romantic in me happily hands over my tote.

"We'll be fine, Lucy. Go call for help." Will leans in close and whispers, "Keep your eye on Wayne. He might be a victim here, but I still don't trust him."

I nod. My thoughts exactly.

Victor looks over our little group. "Now let's find Captain Kip and Bonnie."

Phoebe leans against a palm tree to catch her breath. "Are we there yet?"

The heat and humidity are getting to me, too, but it's the third time she's asked that question. Now I know how my parents felt on all those family road trips when Sebastian and I would grumble from the back seat of the family minivan.

"Do we look like we're there yet?" Wayne snaps at her.

Victor gives Wayne the stink eye. "No need to be snippy, young man. We're all dealing with this the best we know how." He pats Phoebe on the back. "I know this has been rough on you."

"Phoebe is right," Amber says. "We should have reached the boat by now. Maybe we should retrace our steps."

"Good idea," Victor says.

"What's that going to do?" Wayne asks. "I might have been the one who got hit on the head, but you're the ones who are delusional." He glances up at the sky. "It must be close to lunchtime. Is anyone else hungry?"

Phoebe tosses him an accusatory look. "How can you think of food after what's happened?"

"Wasn't everyone supposed to meet near the brook at noon?" I ask. "Maybe Captain Kip is there now setting up the picnic lunch."

Amber nods. "Oh, yes. The professor made sure to tell Captain Kip that we would need lunch. He's very thoughtful that way. I mean, he *was* thoughtful." She sniffles. "I still can't believe he's gone."

Victor uses the back of his hand to blot the sweat from his brow. "Let's keep going." He points to a palm tree. "I'm certain I recognize this tree."

"Really?" Wayne snorts. "How can you tell?" You'd think being hit on the head would have knocked some of the sarcasm out of Wayne, but nope. He's still as disagreeable as ever. I notice, however, that he doesn't seem to be slurring his words as much.

Victor's eyes flare dangerously. "It's too bad that fall on the head didn't knock some civility into you."

"For the hundredth time, I didn't fall. I was attacked," Wayne says. He points to my dog. "You there, do something. Can't you sniff your way back to the boat?"

Paco looks at Wayne the same way he looks at the mail carrier. *Doesn't this cretin know that I'm no ordinary dog?*

I can't help but grin.

Wayne narrows his eyes. "I could swear that dog is thinking something nasty about me."

If he only knew ... I open my mouth to respond to Wayne when a woman's voice cuts through the air. *"Yoo-hoo!* Is anyone out there?"

Victor's eyes light up. "It's Bonnie!"

"Over here!" I shout.

Bonnie emerges from a thick area of brush. And ... yes! Captain Kip is with her. He's laden down with a large cooler, a tackle box, and a fishing pole.

"We were worried about you," Victor says. "I'm afraid we have some terrible news."

"We came across Will and Brittany, so we know about the professor," Captain Kip says grimly. "Damn shame about the old guy. In all my years running excursions, nothing like this has ever happened."

"Where have you been all this time?" I ask Bonnie.

"Apparently, I have no sense of direction. Phoebe and Dr. Drake wanted some privacy, so I wandered around for a bit exploring the island, but I could never find my way back to them. Luckily, I stumbled across Captain Kip fishing, and he offered to help me rejoin the group. That's when we found Will and Brittany and Dr. Drake's body." She shudders. "Thank goodness Captain Kip had a tarp in his fishing gear to cover the poor man. The whole thing is just so horrible."

The hair on my neck stands on edge. Bonnie has just lied to me. But about what? And why on earth would Phoebe and Professor Drake want privacy?

Captain Kip looks at me. "Will says you suspect foul play in the professor's death."

"It certainly looks that way. We were trying to get to the boat so we could call the Coast Guard."

He frowns. "Is that really necessary?"

"Absolutely," Victor says. "We need to notify the authorities as soon as possible."

"So you're just giving up on your expedition?" Captain Kip persists. "Is that what Professor Drake would have wanted? He rented the boat for the whole day. Seems like a waste of his money, if you ask me."

Bonnie nods vigorously. "Captain Kip is right. You know the old saying, 'The show must go on.' I didn't know Dr. Drake, but it seems to me he would have wanted us to continue with his work."

"I can't believe what I'm hearing," Phoebe says. "You people are heartless."

"Regardless of what Dr. Drake might have wanted, it doesn't change the fact that Wayne needs to be seen by a doctor," Victor says. "Not to mention that someone on this island is a murderer. While the idea of finding Lazy Eye Louie's remains is certainly tempting, the sooner we get off this island, the better."

"But—"

Victor cuts Captain Kip off. "I'm going to have to insist that you take us back to the boat at once, sir."

"Oh, all right," Captain Kip grumbles. "Follow me." He leads us through a thick portion of brush, forcing us to move in a single-file line. Luckily, none of those horrible Mexican tree squirrels come along to distract Paco.

We walk long enough that now I'm the one who stops to lean against a tree to catch her breath. "Are you sure you're going in the right direction?"

"It's just a little farther over that way," he says vaguely.

If my neck wasn't so damp from the sweat, the hair would stick out straight. Captain Kip is purposely leading us in circles. But why? What is he trying to hide? I decide to call him out. "I think you're taking us on a wild goose chase."

"I have to agree with Lucy," Victor says. "You'd think a man with your nautical experience would have a better sense of direction."

I turn around to gauge what the rest of the group thinks. Phoebe and Amber both look as exhausted as I feel and ... uh-oh.

"Where are Bonnie and Wayne?" I ask.

Victor spins around. "They were right behind me. At least, I thought they were."

I cup my hands around my mouth. "Bonnie! Wayne!" I shout, but there's no answer.

Paco looks at me. *This is getting old.*

Tell me about it.

Victor points to the ground. "Look there! Those are the footprints we made when we got off the boat."

Victor is right. These are the footprints Will and I followed that eventually led us to the rest of the group. It only makes sense that following them in the opposite direction will take us back to the boat.

Captain Kip begins sputtering something about going another way, but Victor and I ignore him. We follow the footsteps with Phoebe and

Amber trailing behind, leaving Captain Kip no choice but to follow as well. Within a few minutes, we reach the familiar-looking shoreline.

"Look how close we were all this time," says Victor.

"Yeah, but where's the boat?" Amber asks.

Our gazes search up and down the coastline, but there's no sign of the *Feeling Nauti*.

Paco nudges my leg with the tip of his wet nose. *Boat should be right here.*

That's what I think too.

"Don't you have some sort of gadget that tells you where you moored the boat?" Phoebe asks Captain Kip.

"You mean like a tracking device? This isn't *Mission Impossible,*" he scoffs.

We all turn to look at him. His expression of feigned innocence might be amusing if our situation wasn't so precarious. Captain Kip knew darn good and well we wouldn't find the *Feeling Nauti*.

Chapter Ten

I CROSS MY ARMS over my chest and give Captain Kip my best death stare. "Somehow you don't look surprised to find the boat missing."

Phoebe shakes her head like she can't believe this is happening.

Amber starts crying again.

"Captain," Victor says, "we demand to know where the boat is."

Captain Kip puts a hand up in the air. "Now, now, no need for everyone to get their panties in a wad. Gary and the boat will be back by four. In the meantime—"

"Four?" Amber screeches. "We can't stay on this island until then!"

"I think you better explain what's going on," I say.

Captain Kip scrubs a hand down his face and mumbles something about needing a cigarette. "Okay, okay. I double-booked the *Feeling Nauti.*" At the look on our faces, he rushes to add, "It was an innocent mistake! It could have happened to anyone, and there's no harm, is there? Like I said, Gary will be back by four, and I can push the boat even harder leaving than I did coming. We'll be back in Whispering Bay in record time."

Innocent mistake? Ugh. Not likely. Not only has Captain Kip just lied again, but the thought of getting back to Whispering Bay in "record time" has my stomach doing somersaults.

"Where is the boat now?" Victor demands.

"Gary is doing an excursion up the coast, but it's a short trip. Engagement photos or something like that. The photographer booked the boat until two, which gives Gary plenty of time to be back by four. Chances are, the boat will be here even sooner than that. How many photos can you take of two people and a ring?"

Ha! Not only is Captain Kip a dog-hating sociopath, he's also clueless about women and their engagement photos. At least now I know what Gary lied to us about. No wonder he seemed so concerned for my well-being. He must have been chomping at the bit, waiting for me to wake up so he could hightail it back to Whispering Bay.

The disgust on Victor's face mirrors what everyone is feeling right now. "So you double-booked the boat. If it hadn't been for Dr. Drake's death, we would have never found out, would we?"

Captain Kip has the decency to look ashamed. "That was the plan. The good news is, we have plenty of food." He raises the picnic hamper in the air as if it's the answer to all our problems.

"Oh my God," Amber says in a wobbly voice. "We're stranded in the middle of nowhere." I really hope she doesn't start crying again.

"What do we do until Gary gets back with the boat?" Victor asks. "Just sit around looking at one another? We have no internet. No means of communication, and—"

"No toilet," Phoebe finishes glumly.

Captain Kip glances meaningfully around the lush shrubbery. "I wouldn't exactly say no toilet."

Amber's jaw drops. "You mean, you expect us to go to the bathroom out here? On the *ground?*"

Paco wags his tail. *I do it all the time.*

I'm not a nature girl, but roughing it for the next few hours isn't going to kill me. Good thing I packed that toilet paper in my tote.

"Since there's nothing we can do about the situation, I suggest we let Will and Brittany know about this latest development," Victor says.

"What about Wayne and Bonnie?" Phoebe asks, her gaze scanning the island. "Do you think they're all right?"

"Please don't concern yourself with them, Phoebe," Victor says soothingly. "I'm sure they're perfectly capable of taking care of themselves." He turns to Captain Kip. "As for you, sir, I'm extremely disappointed in you, Captain."

I couldn't have said it better myself.

I must say, this is a side of Victor I've never seen before. Ever since we've found Dr. Drake's body, he's been quite the take-charge guy. And extremely solicitous of Phoebe too. But then, they've been friends forever. I'm sure he must be fond of her. Someone has to be, right?

We make our way back to where we left Brittany and Will. A blue tarp covers Professor Drake's body. And lo and behold, Bonnie and Wayne are here too. Something tells me they didn't get lost and just end up back here accidentally. Nope. They purposely gave us the slip to return to the scene of the crime. But why? What are they up to?

"What's going on?" Will asks. "I thought you were going to radio for help."

"The boat is gone," Amber says. "And it's not coming back until four."

Captain Kip tells them about the accidental overbooking. Accidental, my gluteus maximus, but I keep my mouth shut and let him dig himself deeper. He's going to be sorely disappointed if he's expecting anyone here to give Feeling Nauti Excursions a favorable review on his website.

"It looks like we have no choice but to stay here then," Bonnie says, not even trying to hide the glee in her voice.

"You don't sound too unhappy about that," I say, wondering what gives.

"Look," Wayne says, "we're sorry for the old guy. And if we could have channeled the spirit of the dead pirate, it would have made great TV. But maybe we have something even better here."

Phoebe looks taken aback. "Better? What are you talking about?"

"Don't you see?" Wayne says. "We all agree that Dr. Drake was murdered. And by one of us. And now we're all stuck here on this island for the next four hours. It's just like that Agatha Christie novel. What's it called ..."

"And Then There Were None," Will says gloomily.

Wayne snaps his fingers. "Yeah! That's it. Think about it. This could be great! Even better than *The Blair Witch Project.*"

I snort-laugh. "You can't be serious."

"Oh, believe me, Lucy, Wayne and I are dead serious," Bonnie says.

"Can we please stop using words like *dead* and *murdered,*" Amber pleads, her voice shaky.

Brittany consoles her by putting an arm around her shoulder. "This must be hardest of all on you."

Amber nods. "The professor was so excited about the possibility of finding Lazy Eye Louie's spirit. This isn't at all how I imagined today going."

Victor scratches the top of his head like he's confused. "Wasn't *The Blair Witch Project* a documentary about a bunch of teenagers in the woods trying to find the ghost of a deceased witch?"

"It wasn't real," I say. "They just pretended it was a documentary."

"It was so scary," Brittany says. "I couldn't sleep for days after watching it."

"The point being, the film made millions and millions," Wayne says. "Just think what a real documentary about a *real* murder could rake in." He lifts his camera and starts filming. "Here we are, alone, on a deserted island," he narrates in a deep voice. He pans the camera to our faces. "When we stepped off the boat, there were ten of us. Now we're down to nine, with one of us, a ruthless killer, hiding in plain sight."

Paco makes a little sound of disgust. *What am I? Chopped liver?*

"Technically, that would be nine and half," I say, sticking up for my dog.

Will snatches the camera from Wayne's hands. "Not so fast, my friend."

"Hey! Give me back my camera," Wayne snarls. "You have no right to tell me what I can do." It occurs to me that Wayne now sounds completely normal and not all loopy like he did before. Could he have recovered that quickly from a concussion? Or … could he have faked being hit on the head? But if Wayne was faking, wouldn't I have picked up on that?

Brittany stares at the camera like it's on fire. "Will, your fingerprints are on the camera now."

Will looks at the camera a moment, shakes his head, then hands it back to Wayne. "You can't seriously think you can tape what happened here today and try and sell it as entertainment."

"Why not?" Bonnie challenges him. "It's a free country."

The rest of the group looks uncertain.

"What I'm trying to say," Bonnie continues in a more conciliatory tone, "is that we can't get off this island or call for help until Gary comes back with the boat, so we might as well spend our time wisely." She catches my eye and nods toward a nearby palm tree. "Can I speak to you in private?" she mouths.

Reluctantly, Paco and I follow her to the edge of the clearing.

"Did you forget about our deal?" she whispers. "The five-spoon review from the Fussy Foodie?"

"I thought that was in exchange for helping you fake your way through the séance."

"Well, the plan has changed. Haven't you heard of pivoting?" Her expression softens. "That review is in exchange for whatever I need to get a decent piece of film I can produce and sell. C'mon, Lucy, you have to help me. You have no idea what's it like being a flunky to that egomaniac. The Fussy Foodie," she says in a mocking tone. *"Please.* Who calls themselves that?"

As morbid as it sounds, I guess Bonnie is right. It's not like Professor Drake was murdered on purpose to make a documentary. That would be too gruesome to contemplate.

I glance down at Paco. I know he's a dog, but occasionally his opinion is spot-on. "What do you think?"

He looks up at me. *Is a five-spoon review that important to you?*

"From the Fussy Foodie? You better believe it. Look what it's done for Heidi's Bakery!"

Bonnie looks between me and Paco. "Lucy, are you talking to your *dog?"*

Oops. "Um, doesn't everyone? It's not like I'm expecting an answer," I lie, covering up my little faux pas. "What exactly do you want me to do?"

"Everyone will listen to what you say. Haven't you noticed, Lucy? You're a natural-born leader."

"You think so?"

"I've seen the way the rest of the group follows you. If you agree to let Wayne film us for the next few hours, then everyone else will go along with it."

Paco snorts. *I don't trust her. She's just puffing you up.*

"You're just jealous because she can read people better than you," I say to my dog.

Bonnie's brow furrows. "What are you talking about?"

Double oops. "Sorry, just thinking out loud." Nothing Bonnie has said to me is registering as a lie. Okay, so maybe Paco is right and she's using flattery to get me to agree to her plan, but that doesn't make her a terrible person. And just because Wayne is filming all this doesn't mean it's going to be sold as a documentary. Let's get real. What are the odds of some big streaming service like Netflix picking this up? Probably a million to one.

"Sure, all right. Wayne can film us, but he's got to be respectful of everyone's wishes. I don't think Amber wants a camera shoved in her face right now."

"I'll make sure he's very discreet." Bonnie gives me a swift hug. "Thank you, Lucy! You'll see. This will work out fabulously for everyone."

We rejoin the others. Everyone looks at me expectantly, so I clear my throat to make an announcement. "Bonnie and I were just talking, and I don't think it will hurt anything if Wayne takes some footage of the island and of us. We're stuck here for the next four hours, anyway. And maybe whatever he films could even help the police in their investigation. Don't we owe that to Dr. Drake?"

I feel a tad bit ashamed, like I'm exploiting Dr. Drake's death for my own benefit, but the more I think about it, the more it makes sense. Maybe Wayne's footage *could* prove useful to the police.

Everyone starts buzzing. Will looks at me curiously, and I shrug as if to say *why not?*

Captain Kip slaps his hands together. "Now that we've got that settled, who's hungry?"

"How can you think of food after all that's happened?" Amber asks him.

"No sense in withering away. If one of us is really a murderer, then we're going to have to eat to keep up our strength. What if Dr. Drake was just his first victim?"

"Has it occurred to you that the murderer could be a she?" Will says.

"Whatever. He, she ... what does it matter? Besides, if we don't eat, what are we going to do? Just sit here and stare at one another?"

I highly doubt one missed meal will cause Captain Kip to "wither" away, but he's right. Focusing on normal activities will help everyone stay calm.

He tosses another tarp on the ground and starts pulling food from the cooler. Brittany helps by passing around bottles of water and iced tea. It's not exactly the top-rate lunch Gary bragged about, but the food looks decent.

Victor grudgingly sits on the tarp, and one by one everyone joins him, forming a circle. Brittany sits to one side of me and Phoebe on the other.

It feels gruesome eating in such close proximity to Dr. Drake's body. He's less than ten feet away from the group circle, but what choice do we have? Thank goodness his body is covered by the blue tarp.

I take a bite out of a turkey sandwich. The bread is freshly baked. "Where did you get the food?" I ask. "This is pretty good." I have dog food in my tote for Paco, but under the circumstances, he deserves a treat. I break off a piece of my sandwich and give it to him, which he happily noshes down in a few gulps.

"It's catered from Heidi's Bakery. They have a five-spoon review from some hoity-toity food critic. Nothing but the best for my passengers," Captain Kip boasts.

Ugh.

Phoebe, I notice, isn't eating. "What do you think will happen when the police get here?" she asks me quietly. I've known Phoebe Van Cleave a long time. She's always seemed so sturdy. Like a good pair of orthopedic shoes. But ever since we've discovered Dr. Drake's body, it's like she's morphed into a different person—aka someone with a heart.

Sure, we've all been affected by Dr. Drake's murder, but she's taking it more personally than expected. She'd only known the man, what? Half a day? As ridiculous as the notion is, I'm beginning to think Brittany was right when she said Phoebe had a crush on Dr. Drake.

"I suppose they'll want to comb through the crime scene," I say. "Check out all the places that Dr. Drake might have gone to on the island, that sort of thing. You never know what kind of clues they might find."

"Clues?"

"Any piece of physical evidence that they could trace back to the killer."

Brittany joins our conversation. "Won't that be difficult? I mean, we're practically in the middle of a jungle."

"That's why it's so important that Dr. Drake's body be left undisturbed. We wouldn't want to accidentally tamper with any evidence." Good thing I watch *America's Most Vicious Criminals* so that I know this kind of stuff. Being a cop's girlfriend and having solved over a half dozen murders doesn't hurt either.

Brittany's gaze goes to Wayne as she leans over to whisper to me. "Don't you think it's ghoulish letting Wayne film us with the same camera that was used to kill Dr. Drake?"

"I'm sure he'll use that to give his documentary an extra dash of creepiness."

Brittany snorts in agreement.

Wayne films everything, his voice low and somber sounding. "With help hours away, the castaways must now look to one another for survival. All while knowing that one of us is a cold-blooded killer."

Victor frowns at him. "Do you have to say things like that? You're scaring everyone."

Wayne stops filming. "It's the truth. The captain is right. Who knows if one of us is next? Remember, I'm a victim too. The murderer hit me on the head and left me for dead."

Paco lays his head on the ground. *As if we could forget.*

Will puts down his sandwich. "Don't you think you're being melodramatic?"

"No, he's right," Phoebe says. "Someone hit Wayne on the head and then killed Dr. Drake. Maybe we're all doomed."

Amber starts crying again.

Paco looks up at me. *Do something.*

"Can I make a suggestion?" I say. "I admit, I didn't read the book, but I did see the sixties movie version. *Ten Little Indians,* right? I think at some point in the movie, the characters decided the best course of action was to stick together. Why don't we make a pact? No one leaves this circle until we get rescued."

"Ten Little Indians was a subpar version of *And Then There Were None,"* Will says in his best snippy librarian voice. "They even added

a dopey romance, and the ending was all wrong. The book is *always* better than the movie."

"Well, duh," Brittany says, "everyone knows that." Will rewards her with a rare smile, and I'm reminded of my quest to get the two of them together.

Amber raises her hand. "What if someone needs to, um, use the bushes?"

"Then we'll go in pairs," I say.

"That's sound good, except what if you're paired up with the murderer?" Brittany says.

"Then we'll go in groups of three. How's that?"

One by one, everyone reluctantly nods. "That should work," Victor says.

"Only in the book version of *And Then There Were None,* no matter what they do, everyone eventually dies," Will says, causing Amber to start crying again.

I give him a *shut up* look. He shrugs apologetically like the literary snob in him can't help but point out the correct ending.

Maybe Captain Kip is right and Dr. Drake was just the first victim. I glance around at my fellow castaways. Could one of them be a psychopathic serial killer? The amateur sleuth in me screams no. But if Dr. Drake's murder was intentional, what was the motive?

The way I see it, our best chance of getting off this island alive is figuring out the identity of the killer. I have four hours before Gary comes back with the boat. I lock eyes with Paco. *Time to get to work.*

Chapter Eleven

EVEN THOUGH THE ONLY ones who seem to have much of an appetite are Wayne and Captain Kip, everyone eats their lunch. Wayne finishes his sandwich and begins filming again while I think about the best way to go about catching Dr. Drake's killer. Sure, I've solved a bunch of murders before, but each one was different. One thing I've learned, though, is that if I can figure out a motive, I can narrow down my suspects.

Speaking of which, I've ruled out Will and Brittany. Even if they weren't my best friends, neither is capable of something as dastardly as hitting a defenseless man over the head.

I've also ruled out Victor and Phoebe. Victor is a total sweetheart, and maybe I'm being too sentimental, but I've known Phoebe Van Cleave all my life, and while she's a grumpy old curmudgeon, I don't think she could have murdered Dr. Drake. The shock on her face when she discovered that he'd been killed was too real to fake.

Which narrows my suspects to Captain Kip, Bonnie, Amber, and good ol' Wayne. The more I see him in action, running around filming and narrating his documentary, the more suspicious I become. Sure, he got hit on the head and someone stole his camera, but ... did it really happen the way he said it did? Just because I haven't caught him in a lie yet doesn't mean he's being truthful. It just means I haven't asked him the right questions.

If I could just get everyone talking, then I can ferret out who's being truthful and who's lying. The way I figure it, if you're innocent in Dr. Drake's death, then there's no reason to lie.

"I have an idea," I blurt and am instantly met with a sea of hopeful faces.

"About getting off the island?" Amber asks.

"Not exactly. I thought we could each go over what we did once we got off the boat."

Phoebe looks disappointed. "How's that going to help anything?"

"We can talk about our relationship with Dr. Drake and what we did once the expedition began. If we each retrace our movements, one of us is going to have to lie to cover the fact they murdered Dr. Drake."

Captain Kip gives a derisive snort. "Of course the killer is going to lie."

"Exactly," Brittany says. "And once they lie, we'll catch them."

"How's that going to work?" Phoebe says. "It's not like we have a polygraph machine to strap them up to."

Brittany gives me an *oops* look, and Will subtly nods in approval. We have something better than a polygraph machine, and they know it.

Amber pulls a notebook and pen from her backpack. "I have an idea. I'll write down what everyone says, and afterwards, we can compare stories. It should be evident if someone's movements seem off."

"Great idea," Will says. Amber smiles at him. It's a relief to see that she's stopped crying.

Wayne lowers his camera. "I agree. It'll give the documentary a real personal touch." He hits the record button on his camera again and starts narrating. "With Dr. Drake dead, our original goal of finding the remains of Lazy Eye Louie is now on hold with a much more important focus. Justice for Dr. Drake. And for myself, too." He rubs the top of his head again for show. "But this isn't about me. It's about uncovering a murderer."

Ha! Not about him? Clearly, Wayne is looking forward to profiting from Dr. Drake's death.

It occurs to me that in all the murders I've solved over the past year, solving this one should be a slam dunk. I mean, how often do you get all your suspects together at the same time and literally force them to go through their actions prior to the murder? Four hours to solve this crime? Not likely. I'll be ashamed of myself if I don't have this thing solved by the time Captain Kip calls for dessert.

Amber poises her pen above the paper. "Who wants to go first?"

Brittany raises her hand. "I will." She makes fast work of tidying her braid, wets her lips, then gazes sadly into the camera. "I'm Brittany Kelly, the PR manager for the Whispering Bay Chamber of Commerce. First off, I want to say that this island is not remotely part of, or tied to, the Whispering Bay community in any way, so we can't be responsible for anything that happened here. Furthermore—"

Wayne motions with his free hand for her to hurry it up.

"As I was saying," she says, "Whispering Bay, which, by the way, is a lovely beachside town located just a few miles from Seaside and Destin on the northwest part of Florida—"

Wayne turns off his camera. "This isn't a commercial for the chamber of commerce. You're supposed to explain how you ended up on the island and retrace your movements up to the time we found Dr. Drake's body."

"I was getting to that," Brittany says. Wayne shakes his head and begins filming again. "So." She takes a deep breath. "Brittany Kelly here. My very best friend, Lucy McGuffin, and her sweet little dog Paco were asked by the wonderful people at the Sunshine Ghost Society to be part of Dr. Drake's expedition. I insisted on coming here today to help watch Paco. I'm very fond of him, and if anything were to happen to him, I would never forgive myself."

That's weird. The hair on the back of my neck is tingling. Did Brittany just lie?

Paco trots over to lick Brittany on the hand. *I like you too.* She rubs him behind his ears, and he practically melts into the ground.

"So you'd never met Dr. Drake before today?" Wayne asks from behind the lens.

"Nope. The first time I heard his name was last night at Lucy's house."

"Go on," he says.

"After we landed, Captain Kip gave us a rundown on the island, what to look out for in terms of native bugs, that sort of thing. Dr. Drake insisted we put on sunscreen, which we did. Lucy was still asleep from taking the Dramamine and no one wanted to disturb her, so Will volunteered to wait with her until she woke up."

"Don't we already know all this?" Captain Kip says.

"Yes, but every detail is important," I remind everyone. "The more information we can provide as a group, the better our chances of finding out where the hole is. And once we find the hole, we should be able to figure out who stole Wayne's camera and killed Dr. Drake."

"Let's see," Brittany continues, "then Captain Kip showed us the clearing where we're supposed to rendezvous. That's when we broke up into groups so we could cover more area in less time."

"What time was this?" I ask.

Amber supplies the answer. "Nine forty-five. Dr. Drake made sure to note the time."

"Paco and I formed a group with Victor, and we went off exploring," Brittany says. "I really thought with Paco in my group, we'd be the first to find Lazy Eye Louie."

"What exactly were you looking for?" I ask.

"I can answer that," Amber says once more. "Dr. Drake instructed everyone to be on the lookout for any skeletal remains or evidence of a shipwreck."

"We must have walked around for at least half an hour. Or maybe a little bit longer," Brittany says. "That's when the squirrel jumped down from the tree and Paco took off running after him."

"So if you broke up into groups at nine forty-five and you walked around for about a half hour, the squirrel encounter happened at approximately ten fifteen." I look to Victor for confirmation.

"Yes, that sounds right," he says.

"Are you getting all this?" I ask Amber.

"Every word," she says.

"Victor and I took off running after Paco, but we got separated," Brittany narrates for the camera. "I tried my best to find the little guy on my own, but I just seemed to get more lost. Luckily, I ran into Lucy and Will, and while I was telling them what happened to Paco, we heard the scream. We weren't sure at the time, but we know now that it was Amber who screamed. Right after that, Victor found us, and a little after that we found Phoebe."

"What time did you hear Amber scream?" I ask.

Brittany shrugs. "I have no idea. It seemed like I was chasing Paco down forever."

Will supplies the answer. "I checked my watch when you were telling us about the rendezvous time. It was ten thirty-five because I mentioned that you'd be due back to the clearing in ten minutes. The scream happened a couple minutes later, so maybe ten thirty-seven?"

Amber jots this down.

"Then what?" I prompt.

"Then we found Amber and Wayne. He'd been hit on the head, and his camera was missing."

"Can we figure out what time Wayne might have been hit on the head?" Will asks.

"I can tell you that," Wayne says. "I had just looked at my watch before everything went dark. It was exactly ten twenty."

"So," Will deduces, "if all our times are correct, someone hit you on the head around ten twenty, but Amber didn't find you on the ground until seventeen minutes later?"

We all turn to look at Amber. Victor says what we all must be thinking. "That seems like a long time to react considering that the two of you were together."

Amber's face goes red. "I didn't see anybody hit Wayne on the head, if that's what you're asking me."

I wait for a tingling sensation on my neck or some other telltale sign that she's lying, but I get nothing.

"I don't get it," Will says. "How did you miss what happened to Wayne?"

"I already told you. He was walking so fast, I had trouble keeping up with him, and I got lost. By the time I found him, he was lying there on the ground."

"And that's the reason you screamed?" I ask her. "Because you saw Wayne lying on the ground?"

"I had no idea if he was dead or alive!"

The hair on my neck does the hula. Finally! I've caught Amber in a lie. Only it's kind of a strange lie if you ask me. She didn't lie when she said she didn't see Wayne get hit on the head or even that she got lost. But something about her last statement doesn't ring true. And seventeen minutes seems like a long time to wander around lost. What was she doing that whole time?

My Spidey sense happily supplies the answer: Hitting Dr. Drake on the head with Wayne's camera, that's what she was doing. Only, what's her motive? Plus, she seems genuinely upset over Dr. Drake's death. All her crying was definitely real.

"Okay." I recap Amber's version of events. "You're all alone and lost wandering through the brush, when someone comes along and hits Wayne on the head and steals his camera. You find Wayne around ten thirty-seven and you let out a scream that Will, Brittany, and I all hear."

"Don't forget, I heard it too," Victor says.

We turn to look at the rest of our group.

Phoebe and Bonnie both nod.

"You'd have to be deaf not to have heard her scream," Captain Kip grumbles.

"If we all heard Amber scream, we must have all been in close proximity to one another," I say.

"It depends on what you consider close," says Captain Kip. "The island isn't that big, and loud sounds tend to carry easily due to the breeze."

"After you screamed, how long would you say it took us to reach you?" I ask Amber.

"It seemed like forever," she says, "because just seeing him lying there was so terrifying. But I guess it was just a few minutes, maybe."

"Shall we say ten forty?" Since no one objects, I continue, "From there it was just another couple of minutes until we followed Paco's whimpering to find Dr. Drake's body. So from the time Wayne got hit on the head around ten twenty and we discovered Dr. Drake's body at ten forty-two, only twenty-two minutes had gone by."

"We should probably approximate that to twenty to twenty-five minutes," Will says. "Just to be on the safe side."

Everyone shrugs in agreement.

"Which means it took the killer twenty to twenty-five minutes, tops, to hit Wayne over the head, steal his camera, use the camera to murder Dr. Drake, and then somehow make it seem as if they were somewhere else," Will says. "That's a pretty tight timeline."

"Don't forget," Wayne says, "they also erased all the footage I'd taken earlier in the day."

"There's something else we've forgotten," Will says. "What did the killer use to hit Wayne over the head?"

The group looks around, dumbfounded. I'm a little ashamed I didn't think of this before. Will takes a long look at Wayne like he's sizing him up. "Wayne's a tall guy. At least six feet. Someone would have had to hit him pretty hard on the head to knock him out for seventeen whole minutes. I didn't see anything in the area that might have been used a weapon."

"What about the camera?" Phoebe asks.

"I had the camera in my hands when I was knocked out," Wayne says.

Phoebe flushes. "Oh, that's right."

"Write this down," I instruct Amber. "Instrument used to knock Wayne on the head, unknown."

She scribbles it down on the notepad. "Who's next?"

"Will and I were together from the entire time we got off the boat," I say, "which clears both of us as the murderer."

"Unless you both lied about what you did and where you were," Captain Kip says.

"Right," I say sarcastically. "What's my motive for killing Dr. Drake?"

Captain Kip frowns. "What about her?" He points to Brittany. "You and Victor got separated. Either of you could have slipped away and killed Dr. Drake."

"I ... what possible motive could I have for killing the professor?" Brittany asks.

"Psychopaths don't need motives," he says.

Everyone starts talking at once.

I put a hand up in the air to halt the conversation. "I think we're all getting a little punchy here."

"I agree," Will says. "I suggest we go back to retracing each of our steps. Captain, why don't you go next?"

Captain Kip makes a grumpy sound under his breath. "Not sure what I'm supposed to say here other than this whole thing with double-booking the *Feeling Nauti* was a big misunderstanding." He pulls a pack of cigarettes from his shirt pocket and goes to light one up when Phoebe protests.

"Can't you smoke that thing away from the group?" she asks him.

He puts the cigarettes away, letting out a string of curse words that would make even the most seasoned sailor blush.

"Please, Captain, I must insist you refrain from profanity," Victor says. "After all, there are ladies present."

Paco cocks his head to the side. He's not a lady, but I'm pretty sure he's never heard any of these words before. Well ... maybe a couple of them that one time I burned my hand while taking a batch of blueberry muffins out of the oven. Still, if my dog's vocabulary goes south, I'll know who to blame.

I decide to call Captain Kip out on his lie. "Are you sure that double-booking the boat was an accident?"

He scowls. "You calling me a liar?"

Well, yes, as a matter of fact, I am. It's times like this when I wish I could tell everyone about my gift, except most people wouldn't believe it, and half of those who did would think I'm some sort of freak.

"I'm just trying to understand how we got in this mess. Did Dr. Drake book you directly?"

He nods toward Amber. "Amber contacted me on our website, and I got back to her with the details. A couple of days later, she booked the expedition with the professor's credit card."

Victor tsks. "Your system is obviously flawed if it allows you to double-book the boat so easily."

"I already told you people," Captain Kip says. "Gary will be back with the boat in no time."

"How do we know that Gary isn't the one who killed Dr. Drake?" Amber says. We all turn to look at her. "Maybe he killed Dr. Drake and then stole the boat to escape. Maybe ... maybe he's never coming back and we're stuck here until we die!" Her voice starts wobbling like she's on the verge of crying again.

Despite Amber's theatrics, she makes a rather brilliant point. Once Will and I were off the boat, Gary would have had plenty of time to sneak off, kill Dr. Drake, then get back on the boat and return to Whispering Bay for the other excursion. I only wish I'd thought of it myself.

Captain Kip sputters, "You can't possibly think Gary murdered Dr. Drake. I've known him for years! The man is as harmless as a fly. Besides, what motive would he have?"

"I thought you said psychopaths don't need a motive," Brittany says in a falsely sweet voice.

"It's a pretty big assumption to think Gary could have killed Dr. Drake, but we can't rule anyone out. And if it will put you at ease," I say to Amber, "no matter what happens, we aren't stuck here. My boyfriend, Travis, who also happens to be the chief of police of Whispering Bay, has the coordinates to the island. He'll call the Coast Guard if we're late coming back, so one way or another, we are going to get rescued."

Her face melts in relief. "Thank goodness!"

Speaking of Travis, he's going to have a field day with this. I can hear him now: "Lucy, how on earth do you always manage to get yourself tangled up in the middle of a murder?"

As if I could help it! I can think of a thousand ways to spend a Saturday, but dealing with a murder on a hot sticky tropical island full of flying squirrels isn't one of them.

It occurs to me that as Dr. Drake's assistant, Amber knew the man better than anyone here. "Did Dr. Drake have any enemies that you know of?" I ask her.

She takes a few long seconds before answering. "What do you mean?"

"Is there anyone who would have wanted to hurt him? Not just physically but professionally? Maybe another historian who was jealous of his work?"

"I can't think of anyone."

It feels like ants are crawling over my neck. So Dr. Drake did have enemies. Now we're getting somewhere!

Chapter Twelve

"Are you sure Dr. Drake didn't have any enemies?" I ask Amber, knowing full well she's just lied to me.

She stiffens. "Dr. Drake was a kind, lovely man, completely dedicated to his work. There might have been some professional jealousy among the other academics, but no one ever threatened him that I'm aware of."

"How long did you work for him?" Will asks her.

"Six months."

"How did you get the job?" I ask.

"I had just finished my master's degree in anthropology and was looking for something before applying for PhD programs. I've always admired Dr. Drake so I took a research position with him." She starts sniffling again. "He was nothing but kind to me. As a matter of fact, he was going to write me a letter of recommendation."

Huh. So Amber had more to gain by Dr. Drake being alive than dead, but she still lied to me about him not having any enemies. I wish I could call her out on it, but I don't know how to do that without exposing my gift.

Will looks around the circle. "Who's next?"

"I'll go," Wayne says. He hands his camera off to Bonnie so she can film while he's speaking.

Wayne pulls his shoulders back and clears his throat. "I'm Wayne Hopkins, professional documentary filmmaker. I came on the island to film Dr. Drake's expedition, but now, like the rest of my fellow castaways, I'm stranded here with a ruthless killer until help arrives. Maybe I was the intended victim. Who knows?" He gingerly rubs his head. "The killer came after me first. He or she," he says, pausing to gaze at our little group with accusation in his eyes, "hit me over the head and left me for dead."

"If Amber didn't see you get hit on the head," Will says, "how do we know it even happened?"

"What's that supposed to mean?" Wayne says.

"We only have your word that you got hit on the head. Right?"

We all look to Amber for verification. "I've already told you a thousand times, I didn't see *anyone* hit Wayne."

Will nods. "So Wayne could have easily used his camera to kill Dr. Drake, then faked that someone had attacked him to give him an alibi."

Wayne lets out a howl of anger. "I ought to deck you for that!" He lunges at Will. The two men tussle for a few seconds before Victor manages to insert himself between them, barely dodging Wayne's fist in the process.

"See here!" Victor puffs, holding Wayne by the collar. "You're acting like ruffians!"

"What possible motive could I have for killing Dr. Drake?" Wayne chokes out.

"I have no idea," Victor says, "but I'm not the only one who must have noticed you're not slurring your words like before. I have to agree with Will. This supposed attack of yours isn't adding up." He gives the younger men a stern look. "Do I have your word the two of you can conduct yourselves in a gentlemanly fashion?"

Will nods, clearly embarrassed.

Wayne shakes loose from Victor's grasp. "You people are insane. I tell you I was hit on the head and my camera was stolen!"

Rats. Other than a scene fit for an afternoon soap opera, that produced absolutely nothing. Once again, I'm not picking up any vibes that Wayne is lying about getting hit on the head. Coupled with that tight twenty- to twenty-five-minute timeline we've constructed, it seems impossible for Wayne to have killed Dr. Drake.

I have to admit, I'm mightily disappointed. Wayne totally fits the whole Woe-Is-Me-Killer profile. You know the type. The kind who blames everyone else for the bad stuff that happens to him and always has a chip on their shoulder.

"How did you get hired for Dr. Drake's project?" I ask Wayne.

"I did some work for a colleague of Dr. Drake's, and he put me in touch with him. Any more questions?" he asks testily. Before anyone can respond, he motions to Bonnie to hand him back the camera. "Who's next?" he asks, pointing the camera at Will, giving Will no choice but to speak up.

"I'm Will Cunningham, and I'm also Lucy's best friend. I came on Dr. Drake's expedition to help her keep an eye on Paco."

My scalp goes all tingly. *Et tu*, Will? So far, the only people I haven't caught in a lie today are Victor and Wayne.

Will continues. "I never heard of Dr. Drake until last night, and I was never alone on the island. Lucy and I have been together the entire time."

"Says you," Wayne quips. He turns the camera on me. "When we left the boat, you were asleep. How do we know that Cunningham here didn't sneak off the boat while you were snoring, kill the professor, then rush back to your side just as you were waking up?"

Brittany's jaw drops. "That's ridiculous!"

"Why? It's possible, isn't it?" Wayne challenges her.

"No," I say calmly. "I woke up at ten. Your camera wasn't stolen until ten twenty. Remember?"

"Oh, yeah. I forgot," Wayne says, disappointed he can't incriminate Will in the professor's death.

Phoebe stands up. Wayne aims his camera at her. "What's your story, grandma?"

"Grand—" Phoebe's eyes narrow dangerously. "I have to go to the bathroom."

"Now?" Wayne asks.

"Yes, now," Phoebe says firmly.

I reach into my tote and pull out a roll of toilet paper and discreetly hand it to her. "Remember you need to take two other people with you. For safety."

Bonnie gets up. "I'll go with her."

"Me too," Amber says. "I could use a break." She hands the paper and pen to Brittany.

"Stay close and come back as soon as, um, you're done," I feel compelled to call out as the three of them disappear into the brush.

I'm expecting Wayne to turn off his camera, but he continues filming as he narrates, "Three of the women in our party have gone off into the island's thick tropical interior in a sort of buddy system so that no one is left alone with a potential murderer. Hopefully, they'll all come back alive. Stay tuned."

Oh, brother.

"On that cheery note, why don't we take a break from playing twenty questions and enjoy some dessert?" Captain Kip asks. He pulls out a box of doughnuts from the food hamper. Good thing I came prepared with my own baked goods.

"I brought muffins," I say. "If you're ever in Whispering Bay, make sure you check out The Bistro by the Beach, where our specialty is homemade gourmet muffins fresh out of the oven!"

Will shakes his head at me.

Okay, so plugging my café in the middle of a documentary on Dr. Drake's murder seems yucky, not to mention, it reeks of shameless self-promotion, but there's no way I'm going to let Heidi's doughnuts overtake this documentary and get skads of free publicity. Not when she's already got the *Good Morning, North Florida* gig.

All I know is that if the situation were reversed and Heidi was the one here on the island and the captain was about to pull out a box of my delicious muffins, she'd do her best to one-up me with her doughnuts. And I wouldn't blame her one bit. It's not personal; it's business.

We sit around munching on muffins and doughnuts and making small talk, waiting for Phoebe and the rest of our group to come back. But it's taking longer than any of us expected.

Finally, Wayne gets tired of waiting and points his camera at Victor. "Okay, your turn." Brittany picks up the pen and paper to take notes in Amber's place.

Victor says in a grave voice, "I'm Victor Marino, vice president of the Sunshine Ghost Society. A couple of nights ago, Dr. Drake called me and my colleague Phoebe Van Cleave to request our assistance in communing with the spirit of Luis Sánchez, or as he was better known, Lazy Eye Louie. Dr. Drake had recently discovered his diary and was hoping to tie the man to the legendary pirate José Gaspar. I never laid eyes on Dr. Drake until this morning."

"So you had no reason to want to see him harmed?" Wayne clarifies.

"None whatsoever," Victor says.

Uh-oh. My neck feels like it's just been stung by a wasp. Scratch Victor's name off the list of people who haven't lied to me today.

"Once we began exploring the island, Brittany and I were teamed up together, but she already explained how we got separated. Any time I spent out here alone, I was searching for Paco," Victor says.

"Which means you don't have an alibi either, pal." Captain Kip slaps his hands together and rubs them gleefully. "This is getting better by the minute."

"What about you?" Victor challenges him. "Where were you when Wayne was being attacked and Dr. Drake was murdered?"

"You already know where I was. I was fishing."

"Prove it," Victor says.

"How can I prove it?" Captain Kip blusters. "I was fishing alone."

"Then where are your fish?" Victor says, pointing to his gear.

"I didn't catch any," he says stubbornly.

"Some sailor you are," Victor mutters.

Captain Kip turns red, but whether it's from anger or embarrassment, I can't tell. "I don't owe anyone an explanation. I met Dr. Drake when he got on my boat this morning. I didn't know the man. What reason would I have to kill him?"

No one can come up with a retort, so Wayne says, "All right, who's left? Oh, yeah. Muffin Girl." He zooms in on me. Huh. I'm not sure how I feel about that moniker. But if I can call Wayne Man Bun, I guess it's only fair that he calls me Muffin Girl.

"Well, let's see, I'm Lucy McGuffin and—"

A scream slices through the hot muggy air, causing Wayne to nearly drop his camera. "What the—" He whips around and points the camcorder in the direction of the scream.

We all jump off the ground. "Who was that?" Will asks.

Personally, my money is on Amber. "I don't know, but I'm going to find out," I say.

He grabs me by the elbow. "Not alone, you're not."

Amber comes running into the clearing. "Help! She's trying to kill me!"

"This is fantastic stuff," Wayne mutters, pointing the camera at her.

"Where is Phoebe?" Victor asks her. "You didn't leave her all alone out there, did you?"

"I didn't mean to! She went off behind a bush for privacy, but she was taking too long and I got worried. Bonnie went to see if she was okay, but she came back and told me that Phoebe was gone."

"And that's why you screamed?" I ask.

"No. I screamed because I was alone with Bonnie."

Will looks taken aback. "Did Bonnie do anything to threaten you?"

"No, but we were *alone.* Just the two of us! Anything could have happened!"

I grab a cold drink from the cooler and hand it to Amber. "Try and calm down. Where is Bonnie now?"

Bonnie emerges from the brush. "I can't find Phoebe anywhere."

"Well, thank goodness you're okay," I say to her.

She repeats Amber's story, then tosses a chastising look at the younger woman. "You didn't have to take off running. We're supposed to stick together."

"We're supposed to stick together in groups of *three,*" Amber emphasizes. "Sorry, but I'm not taking any chances."

"What do we do about Phoebe?" Victor asks, his voice cracking with emotion. "She's out there, frightened and all alone. We have to find her."

I can't imagine Phoebe Van Cleave frightened of anything, but she has shown a rather vulnerable side during this whole expedition.

Will takes the lead. "Everyone stay here. Victor and I will go look for her. You're okay with it just being you and me, right?" he asks Victor.

Victor nods, clearly relieved. "I'm more than okay with that. Thank you, Will."

The two of them take off into the brush to find Phoebe.

Chapter Thirteen

WAYNE QUICKLY GETS BACK to the business at hand. "Okay, Lucy. You were saying?"

I tell my story to the camera, emphasizing how Paco and I were just doing a favor to the Sunshine Ghost Society by going on Professor Drake's expedition.

"So you had no prior experience with Dr. Drake before today?" Wayne asks.

"Nope," I say, much to his disappointment. I think Wayne thought he'd uncover the motive for killing Dr. Drake with this little show-and-tell of his. As if solving a murder was as easy as pointing a camera at someone!

Wayne has Amber retell her version of today's events for the camera just as Bonnie leans over and confides in a low voice, "I hope Will and Victor are able to find Phoebe."

"What do you think happened to her?"

"One minute she was there, and the next, she was gone." Bonnie gives me the side-eye. "If you ask me, she got lost on purpose."

"Why would she do that?"

Bonnie smirks knowingly. "Think about it, Lucy. What possible reason could someone have to go off by themselves when there's a murderer loose on the island? You saw Amber. She's terrified of being left alone. You know who's not afraid to be out there all alone? The person who killed Dr. Drake, that's who."

"You couldn't be more wrong about Phoebe. According to Brittany, she had a crush on the man. At first, I thought it was kind of funny, but I'm beginning to think it's true."

Bonnie's gaze flies to Brittany. "Really? She told you that? It all makes sense now. Phoebe and the professor must have been having an affair."

"*What?* Where did that come from? Phoebe and Dr. Drake didn't even know each other until today."

Wayne turns his camera on me. "What are you two discussing?"

"It appears that Phoebe Van Cleave and Mortimer Drake were romantically entangled," Bonnie says. "Maybe they had a lover's quarrel and that's why she killed him."

My jaw drops, and Brittany's eyes practically pop out of her head. Geez! Remind me never to tell a Bonnie a secret.

Captain Kip chuckles. "Well, well, well. The old bird is feistier than she looks."

"You can't go around accusing people like that without any evidence," I say to Bonnie.

"Tensions in the group are escalating," Wayne narrates. "It's only a matter of time before the killer strikes next."

This obsession Wayne has with his camera is getting on my last nerve. I count to ten and try my best to ignore him.

"All I know is that Phoebe going to the bathroom was nothing but a ruse," Bonnie says. "The second we left the group, she began acting suspiciously. If she has nothing to hide, then why run away from us?"

I press her for details. "What was she doing that seemed so suspicious?"

"She kept looking on the ground like she'd dropped something. She tried to be discreet, but she didn't fool me one bit."

That doesn't seem so suspicious to me. But I am left wondering what Phoebe was looking for ...

Wayne's voice snaps me back to attention. "What about you, Bonnie? How did you get here today, and where were you when Dr. Drake was murdered?"

Now that Amber is finished telling her version of events, which is basically a replay of what she told us earlier, she takes back her pen and paper from Brittany so she can resume taking notes.

Bonnie gazes sadly into the camera. "My story is different from the others. I'm actually here on false pretenses."

This gets the group's attention fast. "What do you mean?" Amber demands.

"I'm not really a medium. I only posed as one so the Sunshine Ghost Society would invite me along on the expedition."

"I hate liars," Captain Kip mutters.

"Go on," Wayne urges Bonnie.

"My real job is as an assistant to a famous celebrity. I wish I could tell you who, but I signed an NDA, that's a nondisclosure agreement, promising never to reveal their identity." She pauses long enough to let everyone's imaginations run wild. "Currently, I'm working on a media deal for them, and when I heard about the pirate documentary, I wanted to tag along. I thought I could be of some use to the filmmaker, what with all my connections."

Wayne turns the camera on himself. "In full disclosure, I'm the one who brought Bonnie on board this project. We met through a cold call I made to her boss. She was going to help me produce the pirate documentary. If you're seeing this on any kind of streaming service, chances are Bonnie is the producer behind this project."

He turns the camera off. "That was great," he says, beaming at her. "You can't get more real than that." He goes over to the cooler and plucks out a chocolate glazed doughnut. That makes three doughnuts for Wayne today. Not that I'm counting. "How's this for a title for the documentary: *Murder on the Island*. Pretty catchy, huh?"

Bonnie wrinkles her nose. "Too generic. We need to play up the pirate angle. I like *Deadly Expedition*." She turns to me. "What do you think, Lucy?"

I'm beginning to think a five-spoon review from the Fussy Foodie isn't worth having to listen to Wayne and Bonnie capitalizing on Dr. Drake's death.

Before I can answer, Amber says, "You know what I think? I think you and Wayne are both completely gross and morbid."

"I have to agree," Brittany says. "The professor isn't even cold yet, and all you can think of is what title to give your documentary." She shudders. "I don't think I'll get that image of him out of my mind for a long time. Lying there on the ground, his head all bloody."

It was a rather gruesome sight. His long gray hair pulled back in a—my mind takes in the details of the crime scene, and something seems off. "Brittany," I say, "when Dr. Drake got off the boat, was he wearing his baseball cap?"

"The one with the University of Florida logo? I think so."

"Yeah, he was wearing it," says Captain Kip. "I remember because he made everyone apply sunscreen. He made a point of taking off his hat and slathering sunscreen all over his neck and face. Then he put the hat back on."

"He was so considerate," Amber says wistfully. "Always thinking of everyone's health and well-being."

"Why the question about the hat?" Captain Kip asks.

"Because I don't remember seeing the baseball cap when we found him." I make my way to the edge of the clearing where the blue tarp covers Dr. Drake's lifeless body.

Before I can raise the tarp to take a peek, Wayne goes back into action with his camera. "A member of the expedition thinks she might be onto something," he narrates as he films me.

I gingerly lift the edge of the tarp. If I didn't know better, I'd think Dr. Drake was asleep, he looks so peaceful. Paco trots over and takes a look at him. *He's already passed over.*

"How do you know?" I ask my dog.

He's not talking to me.

"How does this work exactly?"

Paco gives me a look. *Don't know.*

Maybe one day I'll understand how all this supernatural mumbo jumbo works. But for now, I have a murder to solve.

"Well?" Brittany asks. "Is he wearing his hat?"

I drop the tarp and do a quick inspection of the surrounding area. "No hat. And it's not anywhere near him either. At least not that I can see."

"What do you think that means?" Bonnie asks.

"Probably nothing. Maybe it fell off his head while he was trekking through the island. Does anyone remember seeing him without the hat?"

"I'm pretty sure he had it on the last time I saw him," Bonnie says. "Remember, I told you Phoebe and the professor wanted to speak alone, so I went off exploring to give them some privacy. She was probably trying to get him to commit to a secret romantic getaway when he rejected her and she got mad and hit him over the head."

Argh. I know Bonnie is playing it up for the camera, but I've had just about enough of her and Wayne. "Isn't there a missing detail in that little scenario? What about the camera? When you left them alone, did Phoebe have Wayne's camera?"

She blinks. "Um, no. I don't think so."

"It's a pretty good-size camera. Could she have hidden it from you? And if the three of you were together the whole time since you left the boat, when could she have snuck off to hit Wayne on the head and steal his camera?"

Bonnie looks deflated. "I didn't think of that."

"Maybe you're the one who's lying about the last time they saw Dr. Drake," Brittany says. "I've known Phoebe Van Cleave my whole life, but I've only known you for a half a day. And you've just admitted that you lied your way onto this expedition. If you lied once, then you can lie again."

Bonnie's face goes red, but before she can respond to Brittany's accusations, Phoebe comes sauntering back into the clearing as if nothing had happened.

"Where have you been?" Brittany asks her. "We were so worried!"

"I was just going to the bathroom," Phoebe says. "There's no crime in that, is there?"

The hair on my head feels like it's being pulled in two directions. Phoebe has just lied to the group again.

"We were supposed to stay in groups of three," Amber chastises her. "You took off and left me alone with Bonnie. What if she'd killed me?"

"What if you'd killed *me?*" Bonnie shoots back at Amber.

Amber looks dumbstruck. "Why would I kill you?"

Right about now, I wouldn't mind leaving the two of them alone to kill each other.

Phoebe glances around the group. "Where are Victor and Will?"

"Out looking for you," I tell her. "Victor is beside himself. We thought something had happened to you."

"Well, as you can see, I'm perfectly fine," she sniffs.

Normally, I'd write this off to Phoebe just being Phoebe, but there's something in her eyes that makes me think there's more to this. I take a good long look at her. That's when I notice that the side of her sundress appears to bulge slightly like she's got something stuffed into a pocket.

"What's in your pocket?" I ask her.

Phoebe stiffens. "Nothing."

Captain Kip frowns. "No, Lucy is right. You're hiding something from us."

Wayne zooms his camera in on Phoebe to catch her reaction.

"I just told you. There's nothing in my pocket! Now I demand that you all leave me alone."

Will and Victor return from their search. Victor takes one look at Phoebe and crushes her into a tight hug. "Oh, thank God! Where have you been? We looked everywhere for you."

She disentangles herself from Victor's arms. "Don't be silly. I'm perfectly fine." I notice, however, that she's blushing.

"We were just about to discover what Phoebe is hiding from us," Wayne says.

"I already told you, I'm not hiding anything," Phoebe insists.

"Then let's see what's in your pocket," Bonnie says.

Out of the blue, Captain Kip lunges and reaches into Phoebe's pocket. She shrieks and slaps him on the head but he emerges victorious, clutching an object in his fist.

At first, everyone is so stunned that no one says anything.

"See here!" Victor stammers. "How *dare* you manhandle a lady?" He has the same look of outrage on his face that Wayne had right before he attacked Will.

Everyone starts chastising the captain and yelling at one another. I wouldn't be surprised if a group brawl broke out. Personally, I blame about fifty percent of our current tempers on the island humidity.

Then I get a look at the object in Captain Kip's hand and do a double take.

It's Dr. Drake's missing baseball hat.

Chapter Fourteen

"YOU HAVE NO RIGHT!" Phoebe snatches the hat back from Captain Kip. "That hat belongs to me."

Victor looks at the hat, then at Phoebe, clearly confused. "Wasn't Dr. Drake wearing that?"

"While you were off looking for Phoebe," Captain Kip says, "Lucy here figured out that Dr. Drake's hat was missing." He gives Phoebe a hard look. "The killer probably took it after killing Dr. Drake. Like some sick trophy."

Brittany eye's go wide. "Oh, I've seen that on *America's Most Vicious Criminals,* haven't we, Lucy?"

We most certainly have. I'm stunned. Is it possible?

Could Phoebe have killed Dr. Drake?

Not five minutes ago, I stood here defending her, but now ... I mentally shake my head. Phoebe Van Cleave might not be my favorite person, but I have a hard time believing she's capable of cold-blooded murder.

"Why don't we start with you telling us what you're doing with Dr. Drake's hat?" I say to Phoebe.

"This is awesome," Wayne says as he repositions the camera.

"I don't owe anyone an explanation," Phoebe says stubbornly. "Now get that camera out of my face."

"I'm sorry, Phoebe," Will says, "but I think you do us an explanation. We all agreed to stay together in groups of at least three. Victor and I just spent the last fifteen minutes combing the area for you. You had us really worried. Especially Victor."

"The thought of Phoebe killing Dr. Drake is utterly ridiculous," Victor says. "I can personally vouch that Phoebe is incapable of any sort of violence."

"Which means squat," Captain Kip says. "How do we know you and Phoebe didn't kill Dr. Drake together? Maybe you're her accomplice!"

Everyone starts talking over each other. Wayne is practically salivating with this new theory. He pans his camera around the group. You can almost see the dollar signs reflected in his eyes.

Phoebe's expression remains stony. Victor goes to her side and places his hand on her elbow. "Phoebe, please. It's important we know how you managed to get Dr. Drake's hat. Whatever you tell us, we'll believe, because in all the years I've known you, you're the most honest person I've ever met."

She blinks in surprise. "Victor, I ..." She shakes her head. "It's personal," she whispers.

"It won't be personal for long," I tell her. "Once the police get here, they'll find out about the hat and they'll want to question you. So you might as well tell us."

"I feel very foolish telling you how I got this hat," she says, not meeting anyone's gaze.

Victor smiles gently. "You're many things, Phoebe Van Cleave, but foolish isn't one of them."

If I didn't know any better, I'd think Victor has *feelings* for Phoebe.

After a few long seconds, she says, "Very well. Lucy's right. It will get out sooner or later. Professor Drake and I were lovers."

The color drains from Victor's face. "But ... you just met the man this morning." He glances around the shrubs like he's imagining ... *ew*. I'm imagining it, too, and it's an image I could have happily skipped, thank you.

"I knew it!" Bonnie says. "It's always the scorned lover. What did he do? Reject you? Is that why you killed him?"

"I did *not* kill Mortimer," Phoebe declares emphatically. "Mortimer and I were students at the University of Florida back in the seventies. We met one night at a frat party. He was so engaging! So different from the other boys. We spent an entire night talking about all the things we had in common—our love of history, hot dogs without mustard, The Who."

Amber blinks. "The who what?"

"Um, I believe that's a popular rock band from the seventies," Will says.

"One thing led to another," Phoebe continues. "You can probably guess the rest. We shared one glorious night of passion. We met for coffee a few days later, but shortly afterward, Mortimer left to spend a semester abroad, and we lost touch. There was no such thing as cell phones back then.

"I never thought of him again, well, hardly ever, until he called the number for the society leaving a message asking for assistance on the expedition. Since I've never married, my name has always remained the same, and I was hoping ..." She shrugs wistfully. "We were like two ships that passed in the night. Our love simply wasn't aligned with the stars."

Oh my. I bite my bottom lip to keep from giggling. I would never want Phoebe to think I was making light of her feelings for Dr. Drake, but that was rather colorful.

Brittany's eyes go all warm. "That's *so* romantic."

"Mortimer had one big love—his work. There was no room for a wife or family. His research was everything to him. When I saw him this morning at the dock and I realized he didn't remember me, I was devastated."

Brittany puts her arm around Phoebe's shoulder. "Of course you were!"

"So that's why you asked me to give the two of you some privacy?" Bonnie says. "So you could remind him of who you were?"

"Yes." Phoebe pauses. "But not to embarrass him or put him on the spot."

"And ... did he remember you?" Victor asks.

"Not at first, but once I reminded him of the details, he remembered. I think he was shocked. But then we had a lovely conversation and he filled me in on what he'd been up to and I told him all about my teaching career and my life in Whispering Bay. He seemed very touched by our reunion, and he wanted to give me a memento to remember him by."

"The hat?" I ask her.

Phoebe nods. "It seemed fitting since we met at university. After our talk, we both needed a few minutes alone to gather ourselves before continuing on with the expedition. I took the hat and found a lovely little spot nearby to think about our conversation." Her eyes go damp. "I never saw Mortimer alive again."

Captain Kip narrows his eyes suspiciously. "So what's that got to do with you sneaking off from the group?"

"It wasn't until after we'd started eating lunch that I realized I must have dropped the hat somewhere on the island. I couldn't leave it out there, so I went to search for it."

"And we're supposed to believe all that?" Captain Kip says.

"It's the truth! I would never do anything to hurt Mortimer."

I let out a huge sigh of relief. Phoebe isn't lying. Not that I thought she was the killer, but it's good to have her name cleared. It would be a real bummer to see her arrested for killing an old college flame. Not to mention what it could do to the dynamics of the Sunshine Ghost Society. Sure, they can be pains in my tushes with all their special orders, but as some of my best customers, I have a lot of affection for them.

I catch Will and Brittany's eye. "I think Phoebe is telling the truth," I say to the group. "Which means we can eliminate her as the killer."

"Says you," Captain Kip growls. "Until we get a confession, I'm not ruling anyone out."

"I think I know who killed Mortimer," Phoebe says.

We all turn to look at her. "Who?" I ask.

Phoebe juts her chin out. "While Mortimer and I were having our private conversation, someone was spying on us. Take that information and do with it what you will."

"That doesn't answer the question," Will says. "Who was spying on you?"

"Who do you think?" Phoebe says coldly. "Oh, she pretended to give us time alone, but all the while she was hiding in the bushes, listening to our conversation."

"Me?" Bonnie screeches. "That's ridiculous! I wanted to produce Dr. Drake's pirate documentary. Why on earth would I want to kill him?"

"Because he didn't want to sell the documentary to Netflix, that's why," Phoebe says.

"That's not true," Bonnie shoots back.

Yuck. It feels like a spider just crawled over my scalp. Thanks a lot for that lie, Bonnie.

Phoebe's blue eyes are almost glowing. "You think you were so clever snooping on Mortimer and me. I saw you hiding in the bushes. I wanted to scream and tell you to come out, but I was afraid if I did, there would never be another chance to be alone with Mortimer again."

Bonnie appears flustered by Phoebe's vehemence. "Okay, so I did stay close by. But only because I didn't want to get lost. I had no interest in whatever you and Dr. Drake were discussing. Besides," she says, "from where I was standing, I couldn't really make out what the two of you were saying."

"That's too bad," Phoebe says, "because that lovely little spot where I went off to be alone? It was downwind from where you and Mortimer had your argument. I heard everything the two of you said to one another."

Bonnie's face goes ashen. "I ... you couldn't have heard what we said."

"Oh no?" Phoebe motions to Wayne to place the camera on her. "This is Phoebe Van Cleave. President of the Sunshine Ghost Society, retired educator, Whispering Bay High School Teacher of the Year in 2008." She frowns. "Or was it 2009? Oh, well. What I'm about to reveal is the truth, the whole truth, and nothing but the truth."

The entire group is riveted. "Go on," Wayne croaks, his voice thick with excitement.

"As it's already been explained, once we reached the island, we broke up into groups. Dr. Drake, myself, and Bonnie whatever-her-name-is," Phoebe says, glaring at Bonnie, "formed one group. It was clear to me from the start that the woman had an agenda."

"How so?" Will asks.

"She kept pestering Mortimer with all sorts of questions about his plans for the documentary. Poor man. All he wanted was to lead a scientific quest to find evidence that José Gaspar once existed. Mortimer was too polite to tell her to shut up. I, however, was not so polite. I told Bonnie I wanted some time alone with Mortimer, and he gladly went along with it so she would leave him alone."

Amber is scribbling like a fiend. "So that's when she left to give you and the professor some privacy?"

Phoebe nods. "We were right in the middle of our conversation when I spotted her. That bright red scarf of hers stood out like a sore thumb against all the greenery. But like I said, I ignored her. After Mortimer and I talked, I went to find a private spot. That's when I turned the tables on her and spied on them. And let me tell you, it was *quite* an enlightening conversation.

"She told Mortimer that her real name wasn't Bonnie Clark. It was Bonnie Albritton and she was the woman who'd been emailing him, wanting to produce his documentary."

Captain Kip whips around to face Bonnie. "Is that true? Is your real name Bonnie Albritton?"

"So what if it is? It wasn't a secret. Not from everyone. Ask Lucy. She'll tell you. She knew my real name."

Now everyone turns to look at me. "Um, well, yes, Bonnie told me that she was using an alias."

"You see what I mean!" Phoebe says, pointing a finger at Bonnie. "If you can't even tell the truth about your own name, how are we supposed to believe anything else you say?"

Amber shakes her head and keeps writing while Wayne keeps recording.

"Let's see," Phoebe says, "where was I? Oh yes, Bonnie told Mortimer that she wanted to produce his pirate documentary and that she had big money contacts through her boss. She wanted to try to sell the documentary to one of those popular streaming services, but Mortimer, being the scholar he was, wasn't interested. He was hoping to sell the documentary to the History Channel or PBS."

"Those channels don't get near as much attention as the big streaming services like Netflix and HBO," Will says.

"I bet they don't pay as well either," Victor says.

"They began to argue," Phoebe continues. "I thought about stepping in and making my presence known, but Mortimer was holding his own against her. He told Bonnie in no uncertain terms that he would never allow her to produce his documentary—"

"That's a lie!" Bonnie says. "Professor Drake was absolutely thrilled by the thought of selling his documentary to a big platform."

Ouch. Bonnie's lie is so big, it's a miracle there's still a hair left on my head.

"Unfortunately, we only have your word on that," I say.

Wayne angles his camera to get a better view of Bonnie's reaction. She places her palm out to block the lens. "Get that thing out of my face! Turn it off. Now!"

Thankfully, Wayne puts the camera down. Not that I'm on Bonnie's side in this. She's clearly lied about her encounter with Dr. Drake, but I'm pretty sure if Wayne hadn't agreed to stop filming, we'd be in the middle of a WWE smackdown.

"As I was saying before I was so rudely interrupted," Phoebe says, "Mortimer wanted nothing to do with Bonnie *or* her vision for his documentary. After all that happened between us, I needed to stretch my legs, so I went for a stroll." Her voice quivers. "If only I had stepped in while he and Bonnie were arguing. Perhaps I could have saved his life."

"You're insane," Bonnie says to Phoebe. "Or senile. Take your pick."

"See here!" Victor interjects. "I've had just about enough of you. Apologize to Phoebe immediately."

Bonnie's face darkens. "I'll do no such thing."

We all stare at one another in stony silence.

"Clearly, we aren't getting anywhere," Victor says finally. "I don't know about anyone else, but I say we stop this ridiculous recording and wait for Gary to get back so we can radio for help."

The rest of the group mumbles their agreement.

Wayne puts his camera away. "In that case, I'm getting another doughnut."

"Lucy," Will says, giving me a pointed look. "Can I talk to you for a few minutes? Alone?"

Paco barks to get Will's attention.

"You too, Paco," he adds with a grin.

Paco and I start to follow Will to the edge of the clearing when Amber reminds us about our buddy system. "Either stay where everyone can see you or you'll need a third person. And the dog doesn't count."

Paco makes a *pfft* sound under his breath. *Excuse me?*

Brittany rises and dusts off the seat of her pants. "I'll go with them."

The three of us, four if you include my dog, find a spot far enough away from the group that they can't hear our conversation. Will is the first to speak. "What do you think, Lucy? Have you caught anyone in a lie yet?"

Chapter Fifteen

HAVE I CAUGHT ANYONE in a lie?

"Just about everyone," I tell them. "Except Wayne."

Brittany blows out a breath. "Really? That's too bad. I was hoping he was the killer."

"Phoebe was telling the truth when she said Dr. Drake didn't want Bonnie producing his pirate video and selling it to a big commercial company. I'm sure Wayne couldn't have been too happy with that news."

"So both Bonnie and Wayne had a motive to kill Dr. Drake, but what about opportunity?" Will asks. Then he frowns like he's just thought of something. "Did you just say *everyone* has lied to you today? You mean everyone except Brittany and me, right?"

"I mean *everyone*. Even Victor told a fib." The guilty looks on their faces make me chuckle. "Don't worry. Neither of you told a big lie, but you both fudged about the reason you came on the expedition."

They sneak a peek at one another, probably wondering what the other one lied about it. "Honestly, it was no big deal," I repeat.

Will looks at his watch. "So we've basically wasted the last two hours of our lives giving Wayne footage for his murder documentary."

"Ugh." Brittany shudders. "He's horrible. I can't believe he attacked you," she says to Will. "Lucy, are you sure Wayne isn't the murderer?"

"I have no idea. I just know that so far, he hasn't lied to me. He really was hit on the head and had his camera stolen. At least, that's what he believes happened."

"That still doesn't clear him of Dr. Drake's murder," Will says. "We only think that Wayne's camera is the murder weapon because it was found so close to Dr. Drake's body and had blood on it."

Brittany's gaze turns shrewd. "Will might be onto something. Maybe the murderer planted the camera under the palm fronds to lead us off the track. You have to admit, it was a terrible hiding place."

"If the camera isn't the murder weapon, then what is?" I ask. "So far the only person I can completely clear of this crime is Phoebe. She wasn't lying when she said she would never hurt Dr. Drake." I shrug. "I thought this murder would be easy to solve, but I'm more confused now than ever."

"You're not the only one who's confused," Will says. "Who would have guessed that Phoebe and Dr. Drake were an item way back in the day?"

Brittany sighs dreamily. "I was really touched by their love story."

"Love story?" Will snorts. "It seemed more like a college one-night stand to me."

"Just because they only shared one night together doesn't mean it wasn't highly meaningful to both of them," Brittany says.

"Yeah, it was so meaningful he got out of the country as quick as he could." Will chuckles. "Can't say I blame him."

"Obviously, we heard two different versions of events," Brittany says tightly.

Uh-oh. Paco and I exchange a look.

Like a typical man, Will remains oblivious to Brittany's feelings. "No, we heard the same story. They hooked up and hadn't seen each other for like a hundred years. What's so touching about that?"

"Just because the professor's life went on without her doesn't discount Phoebe's feelings. For all we know, he was the love of her life."

"Doesn't sound like much of a life," Will mumbles.

Brittany's eyes flash angrily. "The one claim I shall make for my own sex is that we love longest when all hope is gone."

Will blinks. "Did you just make that up?"

"I'm quoting Jane Austen, you dunce. You'd think a librarian would know that."

Will looks confused. "Are you mad?"

She crosses her arms over her chest. "You need to be more specific. Mad as in angry, or mad as in crazy?"

Oh, boy. It looks like my plan to get Will and Brittany together has backfired in the worst way possible.

I'm thinking of something conciliatory to say when a rustling sound catches my attention. It catches Paco's attention too. We glance up into the trees. My heart seizes, and my breath catches in my throat. A squirrel stares back at us, his beady dark eyes searing through us like evil laser beams.

Before I can stop myself, I shout, "Squirrel!"

Paco begins barking, and before I know it, all hell breaks loose. The squirrel starts hopping from tree to tree like he's Tarzan swinging from a vine. Naturally, Paco chases after him, barking like a fiend.

I take off running after my dog. "Paco! Come back here!"

I can hear Will running behind me, shouting at me to slow down, but I can't. If I lose sight of my dog, I might never find him again in all the brush. Not alive, anyway. Do squirrels have rabies? What if Paco gets bitten? I could kick myself for not securing him better.

After a few minutes, the squirrel disappears into the trees and Paco slows down. I scoop my little dog up into my arms and immediately chastise him. "What were you thinking? You could have been killed!"

He pants happily like he's had the time of his life. Good to know someone is having fun out here. He looks up at me with shiny brown eyes. *Squirrel can't kill me.*

"We don't know that for sure. They're horribly sneaky. Besides, this is an island squirrel. We don't know what kind of diseases they might carry."

Paco continues to catch his breath (I do, too, for that matter) when Will and Brittany catch up to us. "Oh, thank God! You're both all right." She looks at Paco and tsks. "That's twice in one day you've run off after a squirrel. Naughty dog! You could have been hurt."

Paco squirms to be let down. "Only if you promise not to run off again," I say.

Promise.

I reluctantly place him on the ground. He goes over to Brittany and nudges her leg with his nose. *Sorry.*

"He says he's sorry he ran off and that you were worried," I tell her, embellishing his apology a bit.

She crouches down and drops a kiss on his tan head. "Apology accepted."

Will looks on sheepishly. "For what's it worth," he says to Brittany, "I'm, um, sorry too. About earlier. I had no idea you and Phoebe were so close."

She rises to meet his gaze. "Phoebe and I aren't close, but I can understand how she feels. Maybe if you put yourself in someone else's shoes, you'd have a little more compassion for their feelings too."

I don't think I've ever seen Will's jaw drop before.

Touché, Brittany!

I'm wondering if I should leave the two of them alone to fight things out between them when Paco begins to whimper. "Oh no you don't, mister. No more squirrel-chasing for you."

Not a squirrel.

I take a good look at his face. His pupils are huge. I suck in a breath. "What is it, boy?"

He starts walking slowly through the brush. We all follow him. After a few hundred feet, we emerge onto the shoreline.

"I think we're on the opposite side of the island," Will says.

"How can you tell?" I ask.

He points to the sand. "For one thing, there's no footprints."

Brittany gazes around. "Will is right. The trees here are sparser than where we landed."

Paco dashes off down the shore, turning his head every few seconds to make sure we're following him. Then he stops and starts digging in the sand. We all run to his side.

"Paco," I warn him, "there might be sand crabs around."

He ignores me and continues to dig. Something tells me to help him. The three of us fall to our knees and start moving sand around. It doesn't take long before we find something.

Paco turns to look at me with a satisfied look on his face.

"Oh my," Brittany whispers in awe. "Is that what I think it is?"

A skull stares back at us, its empty eye sockets blank and creepy-looking.

A shiver of ice runs down my back. "I think we just found Lazy Eye Louie."

Chapter Sixteen

PACO SITS QUIETLY WHILE we finish digging up the rest of the skeletal remains. It doesn't take long because the grave is shallow. "Do you think someone buried him?"

Will glances around. "There's no sign of a shipwreck. Are we sure this is Luis Sánchez?"

"Well, is it?" I ask Paco. "Is this what's left of Lazy Eye Louie?"

Don't know. Not talking to me.

"He says he doesn't know," I tell them.

"But Paco definitely knew where to find the body." Will looks at my dog with renewed respect. "Fascinating."

"This poor man," Brittany says. "It must have been horrible, dying out here all alone."

"We can't know anything for sure until the forensics people get ahold of these bones. Sure, this could be Lazy Eye Louie, or it could be someone else who's been here just long enough for their body to decompose."

"How long does that take?" Brittany asks.

"Under the right conditions, a body could decompose in as quickly as just a few weeks."

Brittany sits back on her haunches and stares at Will. "How on earth do you know that?"

He avoids her gaze. "I must have seen it on *America's Most Vicious Criminals.*"

"Which episode?"

"Um, you know, the one about the serial killer who hid the bodies near the train tracks."

I've seen every episode of *America's Most Vicious Criminals* twice, and I have no clue which one Will is referring to. Plus, he's lying. It's obvious to me that Will must have come across this fascinating fact about decomposing bodies (yuck!) while doing research for one of his novels.

Brittany's brown eyes widen. "Will Cunningham, did you just lie to me?" Before Will can respond to her accusation, she adds in disgust, "You don't have to have Lucy's gift to always know when someone's lying. Your face totally gave you away."

Will opens his mouth, then quickly snaps it shut again. He's trapped, and he knows it.

"You did lie to me!"

Will rakes a hand through his dark hair, making the ends stand up. Normally, he'd look adorable. Right now, though, he just looks like a man who's tired of hiding something. Frankly, I don't blame him. A secret as big as his is a lot to keep inside.

"I learned about the body decomposition rate when I did research for a book," he blurts.

Holy wow. Is Will about to confess what I think he is?

I hold my breath, waiting …

"What kind of book?" Brittany asks.

"An espionage thriller."

I let out my breath. Yep. Will is going to tell Brittany the truth.

Brittany's gaze shoots between me and Will. "What am I missing here?"

"I wrote a few novels that sold pretty well," he explains. "The research was for one of the books. Maybe you've heard of it? *Assassin's Honor.*"

"Of course, I know it. That's the novel Betty Jean's book club was reading last year. I read it, too, and—are you saying you do research for J.W. Quicksilver?"

"I do more than just do research for him. I also write his books."

Brittany looks more confused than ever.

"Brittany," Will says firmly, "I *am* J.W. Quicksilver."

At first, she looks stunned. It's like that moment when you're watching *Star Wars* (the second one) and you first hear Darth Vader say he's Luke's father. You don't know what to think, and while somewhere deep inside it rings true, you want solid proof.

Brittany laughs nervously. "Am I being punked?" She cups her hands around her mouth to shout, "You can come out now, Wayne!"

"Wayne?" Will says, frowning. "He's back at the clearing with everyone else. Probably thinking of more dumb names for his murder documentary."

"Right. You mean he's not going to jump out with his camera and tell me this is some kind of joke?"

Will shakes his head.

"You're J.W. Quicksilver?" she says as it slowly sinks in. "The famous reclusive author the whole world is crazy about?" She turns to me. "Lucy, what's going on here?"

"Will is telling the truth. He's J.W. Quicksilver."

Paco barks like he's adding his own affirmation.

"Why on earth would you keep that a secret?" she asks Will, then she gives Paco a double take. *"Wait.* Did Paco know too?"

"Well ... he does listen in on our conversations," I say. "So, yeah, I guess he knows."

"How long have you known this?" Her tone makes me wince.

"For a while now. I found out when that con man came to town pretending to be Will ... I mean, pretending to be J.W. Quicksilver. Oh, you know what I mean. The one who was murdered and the FBI came to investigate." Although I was the one who solved it in the end. Just sayin'.

Brittany raises a brow. "I recall the incident well. I might be a fool, but I don't have memory issues."

"Brittany," Will begins, "no one thinks you're a—"

"That was seven months ago." Brittany begins to pace along the shoreline, her sneakers bringing up little puffs of sand with each furious step. "So the two of you had this secret all along. And you purposely kept me in the dark."

Paco barks. *Hey!*

Brittany stops her pacing to acknowledge my dog. "Thanks for reminding me, Paco. So the *three* of you knew all along." She stops to glare at me. "I thought you were my best friend."

"You *are* my best friend. But it wasn't my secret to tell."

"Oh, that's convenient."

"Brittany, if you had a secret you didn't want me to share with anyone, I wouldn't. No matter how much I might be tempted to tell Will or anyone else. I respect you too much to break your confidence. Just like I respect Will."

She spins around to face Will. "I had just reconciled myself to being in love with a grossly underpaid civil servant. And I was okay with that, because you're funny and smart and gorgeous. But now I know you're nothing but a big fat liar who's been laughing at me behind my back all this time!"

Will goes pale. "You're in love with me?"

"I don't see any other underpaid civil servants on this beach. Oh, I take that back. You're not a poor librarian, are you? No. You're an internationally famous author!" The way she says the last part, you'd think Will was a homeless heroin junkie.

I don't think I've ever seen Brittany this mad. Sure, she gets aggravated when Tiny puts too much garlic on the pizza. And there was the time when her nail technician ran out of Brittany's signature Bubble Bath nail gel and she had to settle for plain pink, but that was nothing compared to this.

"Remember, Lucy, when you told me that just about everyone had lied to you about something today? And that it included Will and me? Well, I'll tell you what I lied about. I said I wanted to come on this expedition to help you with Paco. But that's only partially true. The real reason I came along today was to spend time with Will."

I knew it! I try for a somber expression because this certainly isn't the time to gloat.

"You wanted to spend time with me?" Will says, still in disbelief. I really thought he was more perceptive than this, but nope.

"I'm not talking to you. Ever. As a matter of fact, once we get off this island, I don't ever want to see you again," she sniffs.

"Brittany," I say, "I can understand how you feel, but—"

"Really? How would you feel if all of sudden, you found out that Travis was a secret undercover CIA agent? Or ... some famous rock star who wore a mask and no one knew their identity?"

I try not to laugh because the last thing I want is for Brittany to think I'm not taking her concerns seriously. "I get it. I'd feel betrayed. But Travis isn't either of those."

"Because you trust him to tell you the truth, right?"

"Yes," I say, cringing. I can see where this is going, and by Will's expression, he can too. It doesn't look good for either one of us right now.

"Real friends trust one another. Obviously, we were never true friends," she says to Will. She gives me a sad look. "You're right, Lucy. It wasn't your secret to tell, so I can forgive you. Eventually."

Paco barks. *What about me?*

Brittany doesn't need me to interpret what Paco just said. She bends over to scratch him behind the ears. "You adorable little pooch. You I can forgive immediately."

"Great," Will mutters. "So the dog is higher on the totem pole than I am. Don't forget," he reminds Brittany, "you're the one who hates my books."

Brittany looks like she's been slapped. "I don't hate your books! I only said I didn't like them because you were so against them yourself. I was trying to ingratiate myself to you, you big dumb oaf."

Will rubs a hand down his face like this is all a bad dream he's trying to wake up from.

"Look," he says finally, "I'm sorry, Brittany. You're right. I should have trusted you. It's just ... I wrote the first book on a fluke, you know? I never thought it would be successful or that my publisher would want me to write another one. And I thought I could straddle the fence between my two worlds, but it's getting harder and harder to do.

"Just about every second I'm not at the library, I'm sitting at my desk writing." He shrugs miserably. "I don't have time to do anything. I even had to give up my basketball league. Pretty much the only thing I do for fun is hang out with Lucy on Friday nights to watch TV and eat pizza, and even that's getting old."

"Hey!" I say.

"Sorry, Lucy, it's not you, but half the time we're watching the show, I'm thinking about some interview my publisher wants me to do or if I've written enough words that day to meet my deadline. When you brought up this expedition last night, it sounded like a great way to forget everything for a day. And yeah, maybe I was also thinking about a future plotline for a book." He looks at Brittany. "And when you volunteered to tag along, it was like icing on the cake, because I wanted to spend time with you too."

Her expression softens a little.

Will sees it and takes immediate advantage. "You know why you and I only had one date? Because that night I almost told you that I was J.W. Quicksilver. Only ... I wanted you to like me for me. Boring old Will Cunningham who likes to read and hang out on the couch on Friday nights watching real life crime shows. But the truth is, I don't have time to date. I'm burning the candle at both ends, and I'm miserable."

She nods sympathetically. "Anyone would be."

So much for Brittany never speaking to Will again.

"But most importantly," he says, "I can't keep pretending that I'm not crazy about you."

Brittany sucks in a breath. "You are?"

He gives her a slow grin. "Yeah, I am."

The two of them stare at one another like a couple of starstruck teenagers. Any minute now they're going to start ripping off each other's clothes.

Paco cocks his head to the side. *Maybe we should give the lovebirds some privacy.*

"I think Paco needs to go for a walk," I say lamely, but neither Brittany nor Will acknowledge me. They're still too busy giving each other the goo-goo eye.

Ha! Wait until Travis finds out about this. He warned me not to play matchmaker, but like a typical man, what does he know? All it took for Brittany and Will to acknowledge their feelings was some good old-fashioned honesty on their parts.

Paco and I turn toward the water to give my two best friends some time alone. We walk along the shore for a good ten minutes. There. That ought to do it. I'm about to turn around and head back when a flash of color catches my eye. Whatever it is, it's farther down the beach.

"C'mon, boy." Paco and I trudge down the shoreline and around a bend and the image sharpens.

It's the *Feeling Nauti!*

How about that? Captain Kip was right. The engagement photo session must have ended earlier than expected. I take off running toward the boat when Gary comes up from the cabin and onto the deck. He turns his back and bends over to pick something up. A small dark object sticks out of the waistband of his shorts.

I suck in a breath. Holy wow. From this distance, I can't be completely sure, but it looks like it might be a gun.

Paco looks up at me. *What?*

I place my index finger over my mouth, instructing him to be quiet. We slink back into the brush where we can't be seen.

Chapter Seventeen

PACO AND I RUN back to find Brittany and Will, but they aren't anywhere near Lazy Eye Louie's bones. "Where do you think they went?" I ask my dog.

He looks up at me. *Who knows?*

We start walking into the brush, and within a few minutes, we come upon them, holding hands and looking all flushed and happy. I take a few seconds to catch my breath. "Sorry, Lucy. We had to get away from that dead body," Brittany says.

Will looks at Brittany with stars in his eyes. "It wasn't a great spot for a heart-to-heart conversation, you know?"

"Never mind, you two. Guess what I just saw? The *Feeling Nauti.*"

The dreamy look on Will's face vanishes. "You saw the boat? Here? On this side of the island?"

I nod. "It's moored just around the bend."

"Did you talk to Gary?"

"No, I wanted to find the two of you first."

"This is wonderful!" Brittany says. "Now we can radio for help and get off this island."

"Not so fast," I say. "Gary has a gun."

Will scowls. "He pointed a gun at you?"

"No, he didn't see me. I made sure of it. He had the gun wedged in the waistband of his shorts. You know, like you see in the movies."

"Are you sure it was a gun?"

"It was a little fuzzy, because he was far enough away he couldn't see me, but I'm ninety percent sure it was a gun."

"Just because Gary has a gun doesn't mean he's up to no good," Will says. "He just drove the boat an hour and a half across the gulf by himself. Maybe he keeps it for protection."

"Protection from what? Flipper?"

Will looks uncertain.

"Something feels wrong," I say. "Let's assume you're right and he keeps the gun for protection. Why have it on him? And why did he moor the boat on the opposite side of the island from where we expect him? This might sound crazy, but what if Gary never left the island? What if he just drove the boat to the other side where he could hide out? What if he's been here this whole time?"

"Why would he do that?" Brittany asks, but before I can answer, her jaw goes slack. *"Oh."*

"Exactly. There's only one reason Gary would hide away from everyone. He must have killed Dr. Drake."

"But that makes no sense," Will says. "If Gary killed Dr. Drake, why would he hang around the island? Wouldn't he leave and never come back?"

"Not necessarily. Not all criminals flee the scene of the crime. Remember the case of that bartender on *America's Most Vicious Criminals?*"

Brittany recoils in disgust. "Oh. He spiked his victims' drinks before killing them. He was the worst."

"Exactly. He was hiding in plain sight. Just like Gary. If Gary left and never came back, it would be too suspicious. This way he's given himself an alibi."

"But wouldn't the alibi fall apart when it was discovered he never went back to Whispering Bay for the other booking?" Will asks.

Paco looks up at me. *Will makes a good point.*

"Whose side are you on?" I ask my dog.

Paco sniffs. *I'm on the side of logic.*

Oh, brother. "Logic, huh? That's hysterical coming from a dog who sees ghosts."

"Lucy," Will says, exasperated. "Stop having a conversation with Paco and concentrate."

"Sorry, but the more I think about it, the more it makes sense. Maybe there was no other booking. Captain Kip might have made all that up. He lied to me about something. I'm just not sure exactly what he lied about. I bet Captain Kip and Gary are in cahoots."

"On the other hand, maybe Gary did do the other booking," Will says. "Captain Kip said someone hired the boat to take engagement photos, right? How long could those take?"

Here we go again. Do men know *nothing* about engagements and weddings?

Will looks at his watch. "It's two thirty. You and I got off the boat a little after ten. It takes an hour and a half to get back to Whispering Bay, so he could have made it there by eleven thirty. An hour or so to take the photos, and they'd finish up by twelve thirty. Then another hour and half to drive the boat back to the island. He could have easily been back thirty minutes ago. Just because he's carrying a gun doesn't mean anything. Remember, Dr. Drake was killed by a blow to the head, not a gunshot wound."

"So we're back to square one?" Brittany says, deflated.

"Sorry," Will says, "but yeah. For all we know, Gary came over to this side of the island to do some fishing before picking us up. Remember, he has no idea that Dr. Drake has been murdered." He sees the defeat in my eyes. "Plus, what possible motive could Gary or Captain Kip have to kill Dr. Drake? Neither of them knew the man."

I recall my conversation with Gary on the boat. He'd seemed genuinely interested in learning about Dr. Drake and the expedition. Well, rats. What Will says is true. Gary had never even heard of Dr. Drake or his work until this morning.

A rustling in the brush alerts us that we're about to have company. It's Victor and Phoebe. "We've been looking all over for you," Victor says. "What happened?"

"Sorry, the three of us were talking when a squirrel came along and Paco ended up chasing him to the other side of the island," I tell them.

Phoebe glances around. "Is that where we are? Everything looks the same to me."

"Me too," Victor admits.

"We're on the other side all right." I tell them about discovering the skeletal remains and about spotting the *Feeling Nauti*.

Phoebe gasps. "Do you think it's Lazy Eye Louie?"

"Hard to say," Will says. "We didn't find any evidence of a shipwreck nearby, and the bones were buried about a foot deep. Either someone dug a really shallow grave or time just covered up the bones with the sand's natural movement. We won't know anything until the bones are examined by an expert."

"It must be Lazy Eye Louie," Phoebe says. "If only Mortimer were alive to see this. He was only hours away from realizing his greatest triumph."

"It's a tragedy, all right," Victor says solemnly. "We must make sure Dr. Drake gets full credit for this discovery."

Phoebe's eyes mist over. "It's the least we can do for him."

"So Captain Kip was telling the truth," Victor says. "Gary really did come back for us."

"I guess so," I say sullenly.

Victor studies my expression. "Is there something you're not telling us?"

"Lucy thinks Gary might have killed Dr. Drake," Will says. "She finds it suspicious that he drove the boat to the other side of the island." He pauses. "Plus, he has a gun."

Victor stiffens. "Oh, he does, does he?"

"Well, I'm about eighty percent sure I saw him with a gun," I say.

"What happened to ninety percent?" Will asks.

"Okay, so maybe it was more like seventy percent."

Will looks up to the sky like he's praying for patience. "Lucy, did Gary have a gun or not?"

"I don't know. But there was definitely something dark sticking out from the waistband of his shorts."

"Like a cell phone, maybe?" Will says.

Huh. I hadn't thought of that. "I guess maybe it could have been a cell phone." Now that I've capitulated on the gun idea, I give up on the rest of my theory as well. "And you're right about Gary and Captain Kip having no motive. At least none that's apparent, so we can probably rule them both out as Dr. Drake's killer. Even if Captain Kip does hate dogs, which makes him a horrible person."

Paco huffs like he still can't believe anyone couldn't love dogs.

"Good, because I'd hate to think Gary had anything to do with Dr. Drake's death," Brittany says. "He seems so *nice.* He was the one who found some Dramamine for Lucy when she was sick."

Speaking of the Dramamine, it occurs to me that Brittany wasn't there when we discovered the reappearance of my missing bottle. For

everyone's benefit, I recount the entire story, beginning when I gave
Phoebe the pills to when the bottle went missing, and then finding
the bottle back in my tote.

"That's so strange," Brittany says. "I could have sworn the bottle
wasn't in your bag when we looked for it on the boat."

"Exactly. And then it magically showed up once we got on the
island. There were four pills missing too." Phoebe raises a dubious
brow at me. "I know that for a fact, because it was a brand-new bottle."
I go on to explain how Will and I counted out the pills to deduce how
many were missing.

"Why would anyone want to steal four Dramamine pills?" Victor
asks. "It's not enough to hurt someone. Is it?"

"I took two Dramamine, and I fell asleep. Phoebe took two pills
too, but it didn't seem to affect her the same way it affected me. Am I
right?" I ask her.

"I was a little tired," she admits, "but I certainly didn't fall asleep
and start drooling like you did."

Drooling? Who said anything about drooling? Was I *drooling?*

Paco's ears lie flat. *Maybe a little.*

I grit my teeth. "Okay, so two pills could do anything—from almost
nothing to make a person fall asleep. But four pills? I think you could
probably count on making someone really drowsy with that dosage."

"You think someone drugged the professor?" Brittany asks.

"Not the professor," Will says. "He had a distinct gash on his head,
most likely caused by the camera. But Wayne?" he looks at us knowingly.

Of course! I feel like such an idiot. "Wayne thinks he was hit on the
head, but if someone slipped him four Dramamine, he was probably
dizzy enough to trip and fall. And he mentioned his mouth was really
dry. That's exactly how I felt when I woke up too."

"It would also explain why he was down for seventeen minutes," Will says. "He was asleep."

"And why he seemed loopy at first but then snapped out of it so quickly," I add. "He didn't have a concussion. He was drugged."

"But what possible reason could anyone want to drug Wayne?" Victor asks.

"I can think of a few dozen," Will says dryly.

"But how was it done?" Phoebe asks. "Wayne seems too sharp to let anyone get the better of him."

Brittany's face lights up. "It was the champagne!"

Will nods in excitement. "Someone saw you give Phoebe the pills and then saw you put the bottle back in your tote. They must have taken your tote when you weren't looking, stolen the bottle of Dramamine, and then slipped it back inside before they got off the boat to explore the island."

"Except we drank the champagne right before we took off this morning. That would be a little after eight, right? Wouldn't Wayne have already felt sleepy before we landed on the island?"

"Not necessarily," Will says. "I read last night that it takes about an hour for the Dramamine to start to work. I'm no pharmacist, but Wayne's a big guy. If someone slipped the Dramamine in his champagne a little after eight, he probably wasn't feeling the full effects when the boat landed at nine thirty. But by ten twenty? The pills were probably starting to do their magic by then."

"But wouldn't Amber have noticed him being drowsy? She and Wayne were together and ..." Brittany slaps her hand over her mouth.

"Exactly!" I say. "It had to have been Amber who slipped Wayne the pills. She was the one pouring everyone champagne. She was all over the boat, filling up everyone's glasses. And Wayne was probably too busy filming to notice."

"The question is, why?" Will says. "What's her motive for drugging Wayne and killing Dr. Drake?"

I have to word this carefully so Phoebe and Victor don't catch on to my super-secret lie-detecting skills. "When we were going around talking for the camera, I asked Amber if Dr. Drake had any enemies. She said no, but I got the feeling she was lying. Maybe she's colluding with a rival of Dr. Drake's?"

Brittany nods shrewdly. "I did notice she squirmed quite a bit during that line of questioning."

"I imagine Mortimer must have had scads of enemies," Phoebe says. "On account of how *brilliant* he was. Every historian in the state was probably hoping to discredit him. You know what they say about jealousy."

"It's a terrible green-eyed monster," Victor says in an odd tone. I look into his eyes, and a light bulb goes off above my head. When Victor swore to the group he would never harm Dr. Drake, I caught him in a lie. And now I know why. Victor is jealous of Dr. Drake! Or rather, his memory. I can't imagine him seriously harming the professor, but I could see him daydreaming of hitting him in the nose. If only to get Phoebe's attention. Oh, dear. How long has Victor been in love with Phoebe?

Will brings me back down to Earth. "Your theory about Amber would also explain why she didn't see anyone hit Wayne on the head. Because *no one* hit Wayne. He fell from the effects of the Dramamine."

"Don't forget all the champagne," Brittany says. "I'm pretty sure he had thirds."

"So you think Amber was trying to sabotage the expedition?" Phoebe asks.

"She *has* sabotaged the expedition," I say.

"But what about all those tears?" Brittany asks. "Those can't have been faked."

"Oh, the tears were real all right. But just because she's feeling remorseful doesn't mean she didn't kill Dr. Drake. Think about it. Of all the people on the island, she had the most opportunity. She drugged Wayne, waited for him to pass out, stole his camera, then used it to kill Dr. Drake. It's the only logical explanation. I can't wait to see the look on her face when I confront her with this."

"Shouldn't one of us let Gary know what's happened?" Brittany says.

"Good idea," Will says. He turns and gives me the same look my older brother Sebastian likes to give me when he thinks I'm in over my head. "I don't think we should confront Amber with our suspicions about the Dramamine. She's already proven to be unstable. And if your hunch is right and she killed Dr. Drake, we have no idea what she might be capable of."

"Very true," Victor says. "I agree with Will. Best not to stir up the hornet's nest."

Rats. I was really looking forward to squeezing the truth out of Amber, but Will and Victor are right. The wisest course is to lay out my theories for the "professionals" and let them handle Dr. Drake's murder. "So what do we do now?" I ask.

"We'll split up," Will says. "Brittany and I will tell the group that Gary is back with the boat. You and Paco can lead Phoebe and Victor through the brush and to the shoreline where the boat is moored. Tell Gary what's going on. He can use the radio to call the authorities."

But before we can implement the plan, Bonnie comes walking out of the shrubbery. She's followed by Wayne and his camera and none other than Amber herself. Her face is flushed, and her voice sounds strained. "There you are! We've been so worried."

"What are you doing here?" Brittany asks. "And where's Captain Kip?"

"He stayed back at the clearing," Bonnie says. "Amber was going ballistic. She thought one of you might have been hurt and insisted we come find you."

Amber glances back at Wayne like he's about to bite her. "We came in a group of three. You know, just in case."

"In case you end up alone with the killer?" Phoebe says. The edge in her voice puts me on alert.

Amber nods.

"Well, since that would be *you*, then you don't have anything to worry about," Phoebe says with a sneer.

"*Me?*" Amber's voice cracks. "You think I killed Dr. Drake?"

"We don't think. We know. Lucy here figured it all out. Didn't you, Lucy?"

Uh-oh. It looks like Phoebe didn't just stir up the hornet's nest; she kicked it to the ground and stomped on it for good measure.

Chapter Eighteen

PHOEBE TAKES A MOMENT to give her version of an apology to the group. "I know we said we weren't going to confront Amber, but I can't help myself. If it was up to me, I'd leave her on this wretched island forever."

Wayne, being Wayne, turns the camera on Amber. "A member of our party has just accused Dr. Drake's assistant of his murder. Well, Amber, what do you have to say for yourself?"

Amber rears back like a mouse cornered by a pack of hungry lions. "You're right. I did kill Dr. Drake." She starts crying. "I'm a terrible person!"

Paco cocks his head to the side. *Wow. That was easy.*

Yeah, too easy. "So you're confessing to killing Dr. Drake?" I clarify.

"What? No! I didn't *kill* him. But ... I am responsible for his death."

I take a moment to process this. Amber is telling the truth. She didn't actually kill Dr. Drake. Now seems as good a time as any to confront her about the Dramamine.

"Does this have anything to do with the pills you took out of my tote?" I say to her.

Paco barks at Amber. *Yeah!*

She looks back at me with a mixture of surprise and relief. "You know about that?"

"So it's true," Phoebe says. "You drugged Wayne and stole his camera."

Wayne sounds like he's choking. "I was *drugged*?"

"Amber took four Dramamine pills out of my tote and slipped it into your champagne," I say. "The question is why."

Amber is crying so hard now that no one can understand her. Victor fishes a handkerchief out of his shirt pocket and hands it to her. "Now, now," he says awkwardly, "you said you didn't actually kill Dr. Drake. Dry your tears and tell us what happened."

She blows her nose and nods. "It was all Toby's fault."

"Who's Toby?" Bonnie asks.

"He's Dr. Whitman's assistant." At the perplexed looks on our faces, she explains, "Dr. Whitman is, or rather *was,* a colleague of Dr. Drake's. He was horribly jealous of the professor. I see that now. One day out of the blue, Toby asked me out for drinks. I thought he liked me, but he was just using me to help Dr. Whitman play a nasty joke on Dr. Drake."

Will whistles softly under his breath. "The diary of Luis Sánchez. It's a fake, isn't it?"

Amber nods. "Yes, but a really good one. Toby said that Dr. Drake and Dr. Whitman played pranks on each other all the time and that Dr. Drake would know immediately that the diary was bogus. But ... he didn't."

"What was your part in this sick joke?" Phoebe asks.

Amber sniffles. "While I was working on my master's degree, I was involved in an archaeological dig near Crystal River, not too far from Tampa. Toby convinced me to tell Dr. Drake that the diary had been found near an excavation site by a former teammate of mine, and that since he was a leading expert on Florida pirate history, he was being given the diary to examine. I never thought in a million years he'd buy any of it. That's not really how these things work, you know?"

"Poor sweet Mortimer," Phoebe says. "He must have been so blinded by the thought that after all these years he was finally going to discover the truth about José Gaspar, he wasn't thinking rationally."

"Once I realized he thought the diary was real, I tried to tell him the truth, but ... he was so excited. He'd sent the diary off to be examined by a panel of experts. Then he heard about this unexplored island, and one thing led to another. Before I could stop him, he'd put together this expedition."

"So you sabotaged the expedition by getting rid of all the footage Wayne had taken," I say.

"That was the plan. I couldn't let that film get out. Poor Dr. Drake, reading the diary excerpts like they were real. Can you imagine if any of his colleagues had gotten ahold of that film? He would have been the laughingstock of the academic world. I was only trying to protect him."

Wayne rubs the back of his head. *"You're* the one who hit me on the head and stole my camera?"

"No, I didn't hit anyone! I overheard Lucy tell Phoebe the Dramamine might make her a little sleepy, and I thought if you took some too, it might make it easier to sneak off with your camera and erase all the footage you took on the boat."

"So you gave me *four* of them?"

Amber cringes. "You're a big guy."

"So Wayne really did trip and fall," Will says.

"Only because I was drugged!" Wayne says.

"How did the camera end up near Dr. Drake's body?" Brittany asks.

"I have no idea," Amber says. "I wasn't lying when I said Wayne and I got separated because he was walking too fast. For a while I couldn't find him. Then when I did, he was lying on the ground but his camera wasn't anywhere nearby. I thought ..." She tears up again. "I thought I'd killed him by giving him the Dramamine!"

"That's when you screamed," I say.

She nods. "I was so scared."

Will grows pensive. "So you drug Wayne and you wait for him to get drowsy enough that you can access his camera. And it works. Sort of. He passes out, but by the time you reach him, his camera is gone."

"Yes, yes. That's what happened. I swear!"

I lock eyes with Will and Brittany. Amber is telling the truth. "I believe you," I say.

"Thank you." She tries to give Victor back his handkerchief, but he motions for her to keep it, eliciting a grateful little smile from her.

"We're still left with the burning question: Who took the camera, erased the film, and killed Dr. Drake?" Bonnie says. Wayne points the camera at her. "Don't look at me! I didn't kill Dr. Drake. Sure, we had an argument about the documentary, but the last thing I'd want is to erase that film. I'm still convinced I could have changed his mind about selling the documentary to Netflix. And believe me, once I had a contract in my hand, he wouldn't have been able to turn down the money."

"Maybe. Maybe not," I say.

Phoebe looks like she just lost her best friend. "After all this, we're still no closer to solving Mortimer's murder."

"The irony," Brittany says, "is that even though the diary was a fake, we still found Lazy Eye Louie."

Amber jolts herself out of her weepy stupor. "What? That's impossible."

"No, it's true," I say. "We think we found Lazy Eye Louie."

"Show me," she says.

Wayne motions for all of us to go ahead while he continues to film. "I want to make sure to get this all on tape. And no one better try to erase it, either," he snarls.

The seven of us trudge through the remaining brush to get to the shoreline. "Where's the boat?" Bonnie asks.

"Just a little farther down to the right. Once you round that bend, you'll be able to see it." I point to an area of sand that's been disturbed. "Right there. There's Lazy Eye Louie."

The group gathers around to take a closer look at the skeletal remains.

Wayne zooms in with his camera and narrates, "With Dr. Drake's body lying on the other side of the island, the remaining members of the expedition discover the long-sought-after corpse of the bootlegger associated with legendary pirate José Gaspar."

"If only Mortimer had lived to see this," Phoebe says sadly.

Amber crouches down to inspect the bones further. "Something here isn't right."

"What do you mean?" Will says.

"I'm no expert, but I've worked a few archaeological dig sites, here in Florida and around the country, and something's off."

"Like what?" I ask.

She points to the pelvis. "Like I said, I'm not an expert, but I think that's a female."

"So it's not Lazy Eye Louie?" Victor asks.

Will takes another look. "There's something else we missed. Take a closer look."

I lean in and gasp. A small hole on the side mars the otherwise intact skull.

"Whoever this is, they were shot in the head," Will says.

Victor whistles under his breath. "What are the odds we would find someone besides Lazy Eye Louie here?"

A male voice I instantly recognize as Gary's says from behind, "I'd say whatever the odds are, they aren't in your favor."

We spin around to see a wide-eyed Captain Kip, his hands held out to his sides like he's being held captive. Gary stands behind him with a gun pointed at the captain's back. "Ladies and gentlemen," Gary says with cold amusement, "meet Mrs. Gary Olsen. Or what's left of her, anyway."

Chapter Nineteen

I KNEW GARY HAD a gun!

Captain Kip looks ready to strangle Gary. "I'm sorry. He showed up at the clearing and demanded to know where everyone had gone. That's when he pulled the gun on me and told me to start walking." His eyes take in the shallow grave with revulsion. "Is that really Laura? I thought she left you and moved to California."

Gary snorts. "You're so gullible."

"All this time ..." Captain Kip turns to face Gary. "Who are *you?*"

"The same guy who's been embezzling from your company for the past five years."

"That's why we've been doing so crummy? You've been *stealing* from me?"

"I figured sooner or later the algae was going to hit the fan and I'd need a nest egg to make a quick getaway. By this time tomorrow, I'll be down in Playa del Carmen, sipping on a margarita and watching the sun go down. Maybe I'll even splurge and hire me one of those mariachi bands to celebrate my new life."

"So you're not only a murderer, you're a thief," Brittany says.

"You know what they say. Sticks and stones may break my bones ..."

"I don't understand," Phoebe says. *"You* killed Dr. Drake?"

"She's a sharp one, isn't she?" Gary says, still pointing the gun at Captain Kip.

"He killed Dr. Drake because he didn't want us finding his wife's body," I explain to the group. "He knew that as long as we were searching for the skeletal remains of Luis Sánchez that his dirty little deed could be exposed. Isn't that right?"

"Now this one," he says aiming the gun at me, "must have eaten her Wheaties this morning."

Paco growls at Gary, causing him to double down on his threat with the gun. "You there, Fido, be quiet, or your mommy will end up next to Laura for eternity."

"It's Paco!" Victor says, indignant. "Not Fido."

Paco makes a small move toward Gary.

I lock gazes with my dog. *Behave.*

Luckily, he obeys me. For now.

"When I was on the boat this morning and you were asking all those questions about Dr. Drake and the expedition, you must have been freaking out. I have to say, you played it pretty cool."

Gary seems pleased by my compliment. "It wasn't easy." He glances down at the grave. "Laura was going to leave me, but we made a vow. Till death do us part. So I was just holding up my part of the bargain. But then, the big question was, what to do with her body? I thought about tossing her into the gulf, but that seemed a little heartless. You all thought this island was unexplored, but I found it years ago, and I thought, why not give Laura a proper burial? It's what any decent husband would do. That way I could come pay my respects whenever I came out here to fish. The grouper on this side of the island are always hopping."

"My God," Captain Kip says, "all this time we've been double-booking excursions, working our tails off ... just so you can rip me off. I've been working with a psychopath."

"At least I'm not incompetent when it comes to my business."

"No wonder you were so anxious to get Lucy and me off the boat," Will says. "You had already decided to kill Dr. Drake."

"Not exactly. I just knew I had to do something to stop all of you from searching the island. And I had to do it fast because we had a booking to keep." He turns to Captain Kip. "You'll be happy to know that I got back to Whispering Bay just in time for that couple and the photographer to board the boat. So no bad reviews for you. Not that it'll matter soon."

Despite the heat and humidity, I go cold. "What happened when Will and I got off the boat?"

"I waited a few minutes so you wouldn't see me, then I went exploring. I figured a solution would come to me. And it did. I was hiding in the bushes when Bonnie here and Dr. Drake had their big argument. I waited until she stormed off, and I jumped Dr. Drake from behind. It was all over fast. He didn't even know what hit him."

Phoebe stifles a sob.

Wayne looks down at his camera. "How did you get my camera?"

"Your ... oh." Gary smiles creepily. "I used the back of my gun to hit the old guy. A bullet would have been cleaner, but then everyone would have heard the shot and come running. The camera idea came later. I was sneaking back to the boat when I saw you sawing logs there on the ground. Your camera was right next to you, so I figured, why not? I took it and smeared some blood from Dr. Drake's head and buried it where even a moron could find it."

"I knew it!" Wayne says. "I *was* being set up for Dr. Drake's murder!"

"Hey, someone has to pay for the old guy, and it certainly isn't going to be me."

"Why did you erase the footage Wayne had taken earlier?" I ask.

"I didn't want to take any chances that he'd taken some footage of something I didn't want getting out. I wasn't sure how this was going to play out. Not until now."

I gulp hard. I really don't like that last part at all.

"So after I hid the camera under the leaves, I drove the boat as fast as I could back to Whispering Bay." He looks at me and tsks. "You wouldn't have liked that at all. The water was really choppy."

He frowns. "The engagement photos, now that almost messed things up. The photographer was taking way longer than I thought she would. These people were even trying to get me to take them over to Destin, so I made up a story about the engine not working right and got them off the boat. Who knew those things took so long?"

"Oh, engagement photos are very important," Brittany says. "You can't rush through those."

"After I got them off the boat, I headed back here as quick as I could. I thought once the authorities find out about Dr. Drake's murder, they'll want to search the entire island. I was going to dig up Laura and toss her in the gulf so no one would be the wiser. I figured I've been a good husband long enough." He shrugs. "Time to move past my grieving stage."

I bite my tongue. No use antagonizing Gary right now.

"So I went to the spot where I'd buried her, and what did I find? Some clever person had already dug her up. Couldn't very well get rid of her then. So you've all left me no choice. I found Kip eating doughnuts out there in the brush all alone. And then I found all you lovely people."

"What happens now?" Will asks quietly.

"That's up to you. I'm not a horrible person. But obviously I can't have the police here digging up my business. I'll let you all pick. You can go quick or you can go slow."

Amber starts to tremble. "Go quick where?"

He shakes his head like he can't believe he has to spell it out for her. "You can stay here on the island and die a slow and natural death. Or you can come out on the boat with me and I'll put a bullet in you and dump you in the gulf. Either way, no skin off my nose. There are hundreds of islands just like this one. By the time some search party gets lucky and finds the right one, you'll all be long gone by then."

"We take the slow and natural death," I blurt.

Will and Brittany nod, following my lead. "Yes," Will says. "Slow and natural."

Everyone except Amber murmurs their agreement. She turns to me, crying. "I thought you said your boyfriend had the coordinates to the island! You said if we were even a minute late getting back, he'd send the Coast Guard to come find us."

Gary's gaze turns shrewd. "Is that right?"

I think fast. "That was just a lie I made up to make Amber feel better."

Amber's eyes widen as she realizes what she's done. "Yes, yes. Lucy was just saying that so I wouldn't panic."

"Nice try, but try harder," Gary says. "Looks like it's going to be the quick way. It's better for me, anyway. No loose ends to worry about." He waves the gun toward the boat. "Single-file line. All of you. Including the dog. Anyone makes a move and the last person in line gets it right in the back of the head."

"What are you going to do?" Captain Kip says. "Kill me too?"

"Sorry, Kip, but I have no choice. If I thought you'd come down to Mexico with me willingly, then I'd take you along. We've made a pretty good team up to now, don't you think? Problem is, I can't trust you. Besides, the money will last longer with just one person."

"Haven't you forgotten something?" I say. "My boyfriend and the Coast Guard will be here this evening to look for us. Or morning at the absolute latest. They'll find an empty island with a skeleton, and it won't take long for the forensics people to match the bones to your missing wife. Then they'll come looking for you. Travis won't stop until he finds us."

"I've already thought of that. After I dispose of your little expedition party, I'm coming back here to get Laura. Once I dump her in the gulf, I'll be off to Mexico. I'm afraid the Coast Guard will search in vain because all they'll find is an empty island with Dr. Drake's body, a cooler, and some leftover muffins no one wanted. See? I'll be a victim here too. For all they know, we perished at sea. It will be one of those unsolved mysteries no one can figure out." His voice turns low and mocking. "Whatever happened to the Dr. Drake expedition?" He chuckles. "Maybe they'll think we were abducted by aliens. Wouldn't that be a hoot?"

Paco looks at me with the same fury I feel deep in my soul.

Some leftover muffins *no one wanted*?

I gather every ounce of control to keep my tone meek and humble. "Can I ask you a favor? Please don't kill my dog. He can't hurt you. And he's really talented. You could sell him and makes lots of money."

"Sell him to who?" Gary asks.

Victor looks indignant. "Anyone with an ounce of intelligence would want Paco for their own."

The rest of the group chimes in. "Yes, please spare him," Brittany pleads. "He's an innocent dog. He can't tell anyone what's happened here."

Even Captain Kip, the dog hater, says, "You've got enough blood on your hands. No use killing the mutt too."

"Sell him, huh?" Gary nods like he's warming up to the idea. "How much do you think I could get for him?"

"To the right owner? Thousands, maybe even hundreds of thousands," I say.

"Now you're just playing with me," he says.

"No, it's true. He can communicate with the dead. How do you think we knew where to search for Laura's body? Paco knew there was a body buried under that sand, and he knew *exactly* where to dig it up."

Gary thinks it over. "You said he had like a half million followers on Facebook, right? Maybe I could sell him to one of those cartels. They're always killing each other. Bet they'd like to know where all the bodies are buried." He gives Paco a long, hard stare. "Okay, sure. I won't kill him. As long as he doesn't bite me."

"He won't bite you. I promise." I warn my little dog with my gaze. *We'll have a chance to take this psycho down, but for now, we have to play it safe.* "You'll be a good, boy. Right?"

"Tell him to come over here," Gary says.

Paco doesn't need to be told anything. He trots over to Gary's side on his own, causing Gary to chuckle. "What do you know? He likes me already."

Chapter Twenty

LIKE OBEDIENT LITTLE SOLDIERS, we form a single-file line with Victor in the lead and Will at the rear. With Gary's gun firmly wedged in Will's back, we slowly march down the beach. No one says anything. The sound of the water gently lapping against the shore and an occasional sniffle from Amber makes the mood extra grim.

I look up at the sky. The sun is making its way down, but it's not even close to sunset yet. I figure it must be around four.

I think about the look on Travis's face when he realizes the boat is late coming back. Will he really call the Coast Guard one minute after five if he can't reach me? Or was that just the talk of an overly worried boyfriend?

Paco, who's walking next to Gary, reads my thoughts and *pffts. He'll call the Coast Guard.*

Despite the seriousness of our current predicament, it's hard not to smile. Paco is right. Travis will immediately call for help.

But Gary is also right. The only thing anyone will find when they come searching for us is an empty island. The thought of never seeing Travis again, or my parents and my brother Sebastian, wipes the smile off my face.

Not to mention, who's going to make the muffins for the Monday morning breakfast crowd? There will probably be a riot at The Bistro when the customers realize there are no fresh banana walnut muffins (that's the current muffin of the month), and the only person to help Sarah will be Betty Jean. I certainly wouldn't wish that scenario on my worst enemy.

Speaking of enemies ... Heidi will probably be sad I'm gone. For about a minute. Let's be real. How long can Sarah keep The Bistro by the Beach open without me? Her mac and cheese alone would keep our customers coming, but eventually, working the café as the solo owner would be too much for her and she'll have to close our doors. That would leave Heidi's Bakery as the only place in town to get a decent breakfast. How is that fair? She already has a five-spoon review from the Fussy Foodie and an appearance on *Good Morning, North Florida*.

Sure, I want to live for selfish reasons, but I also *owe* it to the citizens of Whispering Bay to make it out of here alive. Not to mention I have to save my dog from a life of indentured servitude working for the cartels.

My mind starts whirling. If we could only distract Gary, maybe we could get the gun from him. There's nine of us and only one of him, so the odds are in our favor. But what if he shoots Will or someone else in our group? Do we want to risk that? At this rate, we're all going to die anyway, so it might be worth a try.

Except now we're almost to the boat. Once we board the *Feeling Nauti* our chances of overpowering Gary might not be as good as out here in the open where we can run for cover.

"Stop right there," Gary commands, and we halt in our tracks. "One by one, go up the ladder, nice and easy, and get in the boat. If anyone makes any sudden moves, I'll start shooting. Understand?"

We all nod.

"Good. Now you first," he says to Victor.

As Victor climbs the ladder to get into the boat, he turns to look at Phoebe with grave eyes. "If this is our last opportunity to speak to one another, I just want to say that being your friend has been the greatest honor of my life."

Phoebe sucks in a breath. "Oh, Victor."

I have to say, this is pretty romantic. I vow then and there that if I make it out of here alive, Victor and Phoebe will be my next matchmaking project.

Once Victor is in the boat, he reaches down to help Phoebe up the ladder. Next up is Bonnie, and after that, Brittany. There's just five of us left. Once we're all on the boat, we'll be nothing more than sitting ducks.

Gary's voice cuts through my thoughts. "Hey! What's up with that camera?"

We all turn to see Wayne holding his camera and filming everyone go up the ladder. "I'm just taking one last shot of the expedition," Wayne says glumly like a man on death row. Which, technically, we all are.

"What for?" Gary asks suspiciously.

"Because it's my job, man."

"No way. Hand over that camera."

"What's it going to hurt if I film a little more?" Wayne asks. "The camera's going with me, right? Who's going to find it at the bottom of the gulf?"

Gary thinks it over. "It could be used as evidence."

"Once it hits salt water, it's going to be ruined. It's not going to be evidence of anything. Let me have a little dignity at the end."

"Sorry, pal. Hand over the camera." Gary motions to the camera with his gun.

"You'll have to pry it from my cold, dead hands," Wayne says.

"That can be arranged. Now hand it over or this guy gets a bullet." He digs the gun harder into Will's back.

Will holds perfectly still. Everyone turns to look at Wayne.

"For Pete's sake, just give up the camera!" Brittany says.

Wayne falters for a moment like he's thinking. After a few long seconds, he capitulates. "Okay, but if I can't have it, nobody can." He throws the camera like a football down the beach, where it hits the sand with a thud, landing a good thirty or forty yards away.

For a moment, everyone is so stunned that nobody moves. Including Gary. Paco and I lock eyes. *I'm going for it.*

"Will!" I scream. "Duck!"

Will hits the sand just as Paco lunges at Gary. My dog sinks his teeth into Gary's right calf.

"What the—" Gary aims the gun at Paco. My lungs seize up. Will manages to kick the gun out of Gary's hand, forcing the two of them to scramble for the weapon.

From a distance, I hear Victor yelling at Wayne. "Where are you going?"

I turn to see Wayne dashing down the sand to retrieve his camera. Captain Kip, seeing Will and Gary still fighting for the gun, jumps on Gary's back, causing both men to fall into the shallow water. Will grabs the gun just as Captain Kip overpowers Gary, placing his arm around the thinner man's neck to place him in a chokehold. "Hold still you, bastard!" Captain Kip yells.

Will points the gun at Gary. "That's enough." He motions to the captain. "I've got him. Go get on the radio and call for help."

Captain Kip runs to the boat.

Paco dashes toward me. I grab him in my arms and squeeze him tight. "Are you okay?"

He barks happily. *Of course I am.*

"You scared the living daylights out of me! But your timing was perfect," I say to my dog. The rest of the group gathers around, shaken but giddy that we've been saved from death and a watery grave while Will keeps the gun pointed at Gary. They all take turns patting Paco on the head and heaping praise on him. Which, naturally, he eats up.

Wayne dusts the sand off his camera and studies it a minute. His face splits into a grin. "It's all still here! All the film I took. It's all good!"

Victor shakes his head in disbelief. "Who would have thought Wayne's obsession with that camera would provide the diversion that allowed Paco to save our lives?"

Paco looks up at me. *Hey, I'll take whatever I can get.*

Bonnie rushes to check out the footage. "Incredible." She and Wayne high-five each other. "This is going to make one hell of a documentary."

Phoebe crosses her arms over her chest. "You can't be serious about that."

"You signed a release, remember?" Bonnie points out. "You all did."

"Yes, but that release was for a documentary to explore the island for any signs of Luis Sánchez and his doomed voyage," Amber says, "not to exploit Dr. Drake's murder. I have all the paperwork right here." She digs into her backpack and pulls out a folder. "Want to read the fine print?"

Bonnie looks at me beseechingly. "Lucy, tell them how important it is that we get everyone's cooperation on this." She glances wildly around the group. "We've just spent an entire day being terrorized by a madman! The world needs to see what happened to us."

"And you want to make money off that," Victor says. "I'm sorry, but I'm with Phoebe on this."

"Lucy?" Bonnie says, her voice pleading. "Remember our deal?"

Everyone turns to look at me. "What deal?" Brittany asks.

I cringe. It seemed like a good idea at the time. But now? Not so much. "I made a deal with Bonnie to convince everyone to go along with Wayne's documentary in exchange for a five-spoon review from the Fussy Foodie. Bonnie is his assistant."

"That's privileged information," she hisses.

"That you willingly gave up. So what if everyone knows you're the Fussy Foodie's assistant? No one knows who he or she is, so their secret is still safe."

"Only now that you've outed me in front of all these people, I won't be any use to him," Bonnie says, fuming. "I was able to keep my job by being anonymous. When he finds out all these people know I'm his assistant, he'll fire me."

Oops. I guess that makes sense. "I'm sorry. But look on the bright side. You said you hated working for him. Now's your chance to break away. If you think about it, I actually did you a favor."

Bonnie's face turns red. "I want to leave on my own terms. Only an *idiot* would think getting me fired is doing me a favor!"

I cringe. "Does that mean The Bistro by the Beach isn't getting a five-spoon review?"

"In your dreams," she says before storming off to confer with Wayne. What they're talking about I don't know, but midway into their conversation, they turn around to give me a dirty look. He's probably telling her all about how one of my muffins killed his ex-boss (not my fault!).

Oh well. The important thing is we're alive.

Captain Kip climbs down the boat ladder with a sturdy-looking rope in his hands. "I just radioed for help. We should be getting rein-forcements soon. In the meantime, I won't feel comfortable until we tie him up."

"Be my guest." Will keeps the gun pointed at Gary while Captain Kip makes fast work of tying Gary's hands behind his back.

"Hey! Be careful. You're cutting off my circulation," Gary whines.

Captain Kip gets within an inch of Gary's face. "I trusted you." Gary mutters something and looks away. "Not such a big guy anymore, huh?" Kip shakes his head. "You never can tell about people. Or dogs." He looks at Paco in amazement. "It's almost like the two of you can read each other's minds," he says to me.

"That happens sometimes between dogs and their owners."

He squats down to get on Paco's eye level. "I was wrong about you, little guy. You can go on my boat anytime."

Paco wags his tail. *Apology accepted.*

"If it wasn't for that dog ..." Captain Kip says, still stunned by everything that's happened. "He's a real hero."

Tell me something I don't know.

Chapter
Twenty-One

THIRTY MINUTES LATER, THE Coast Guard arrives. The first thing they do is put Gary in handcuffs while the rest of us cheer them on.

An hour later, another boat arrives with Travis and other members of local law enforcement. By the time they've collected all their evidence and taken Dr. Drake's body on board their boat, it's full-on dark and everyone is exhausted. We don't make it back to Whispering Bay until after nine. The only thing I want right now is a hot shower, a greasy cheeseburger from The Burger Barn, and my nice comfy bed.

Travis goes to pick up the cheeseburgers while I shower. But first things first. I call my parents to reassure them I'm alive, because this is Whispering Bay, and if my mom has gone to the Piggly Wiggly in the past hour, she knows everything that's happened already.

"Lucy!" Mom says when she answers the phone. "Are you all right? I heard you'd been kidnapped by pirates but the Navy rescued you and ... oh, wait, your father wants to hear what happened. George!" she yells. "Pick up the other line!"

"Mom, I'm fine." She lets me get away with the short version of events, but only if I promise to give her the long version complete with all the juicy details tomorrow night at our weekly Sunday night McGuffin family dinner.

By the time Travis gets back with the food, I'm in my flannel pj bottoms and my sweatshirt that reads *Muffins Rule, Doughnuts Drool* (another one of my personal favorites).

We sit on the couch in my living room eating and decompressing. Occasionally, I'll toss a french fry to Paco and Ellie. "Don't tell Dr. Brooks," I tell my dog. After today, Paco deserves all the french fries in the world. Travis scratches Ellie on the head. He looks almost as tired as I feel.

"Long day?" I joke.

"Not as long as yours. When that call came in from the Coast Guard alerting us to what had happened ..." He shakes his head. "I'll be lucky if I live to be forty around you."

"You know the saying: All's well that ends well."

"I knew you were going to say that."

"Oh! Guess what? I almost forgot. Will and Brittany are together."

He raises a brow in interest. "Oh yeah? How'd that happen?"

"Well, not to brag or anything, but I practically forced the two of them to see what was right in front of their faces." I pause. "And there's something else. Will is going is tell everyone, but I wanted you to hear it from me first. He's J.W. Quicksilver."

Travis's head shoots off the couch. "As in J.W. Quicksilver, the *writer?*"

I fill him in on Will's secret life. "All this time Will was J.W. Quicksilver," Travis muses. "Unbelievable."

"I hope you understand why I couldn't tell you. I couldn't tell anyone, really. Will swore me to secrecy."

"Do you think your brother knows?"

"Yeah, he and I are just about the only ones in town who know the truth."

"What's Will going to do?"

"I have no idea. Maybe he'll fill us in at dinner tomorrow at my parents' house."

"That's still on?"

I swat Travis on the shoulder with a couch pillow. "How long have you known me? Sunday evening at the McGuffin household is sacred. Besides, this is one Sunday dinner I can't miss. Can you imagine the looks on my mom and dad's faces when Will tells everyone that he's their favorite author?"

Travis scratches his chin. "Yeah, it should be a real hoot."

"What's wrong? You don't look happy."

"No, it's just ... I thought we could skip dinner at your parents' tomorrow and go to The Harbor House to make up for the dinner we missed tonight."

"Skip dinner at my parents'? Not likely. Mom and Dad are going to want to grill me about what happened today. Maybe next weekend?" Then I remember next weekend isn't going to work. "Oops. Sorry. I forgot. Sarah and I are completely revamping our computer system, and we only have next Friday and Saturday evening to figure out all the kinks. We can do dinner at The Harbor House anytime, though, right?"

"Sure," he says, "we can do it anytime." The disappointment in his voice makes me feel awful.

"I'm a terrible girlfriend, aren't I?"

He frowns. "What makes you say that?"

"I work all the time, and when I do take a day off, I end up getting into these horrible situations—not that they're my fault—but ... if I hadn't gone on the expedition, none of this would have happened and we would have had a lovely dinner at The Harbor House tonight. I wouldn't blame you one bit if you said I told you so."

"And if you hadn't gone, Gary Olsen would have gotten away with murder." He puts his arm around me and kisses the top of my head. "I might not say it often, but I'm proud of you, McGuffin. You're a badass, you know that?"

I smile, but there's a wistfulness to Travis's voice that makes me wonder if that's a good thing.

Will has been a regular at my parents' Sunday night dinner ever since he and Sebastian were in high school together. Brittany began joining us about a year ago, and then when Travis and I started dating, he and his dad, Jim, rounded out the group. Which is perfect, because our family dining room table has eight chairs and Mom hates to see an empty spot. Paco and Ellie don't count, since they lay under the table. Preferably where they can get the best scraps.

Talk at dinner focuses strictly on Dr. Drake's doomed expedition. "What's going to happen to this Gary person?" Dad asks.

Travis's father, Jim, a retired police officer, takes a stab at answering. "He's got two murders under his belt. My guess is he's going away for life."

Brittany shudders. "Good riddance." Her expression turns thoughtful. "I heard Amber say she's going to continue with Dr. Drake's work. She really feels bad about her part in the fake diary scheme, and she's going to make sure that the academic community knows Dr. Drake had no part in that."

"So much for Bonnie and Wayne's pirate documentary," I say.

"Do you think they'll still try to make some kind of documentary out of the footage Wayne took?" my brother Sebastian asks.

"Not if he doesn't want to end up in court," Will says. "Phoebe Van Cleave is determined that none of that film gets released."

Mom tsks. "Who would have thought Phoebe Van Cleave and Professor Drake? I've known Phoebe for years, and she's never had a boyfriend."

"That might be about to change," I say slyly.

Travis gives me a warning look. "Lucy, stay out of it."

"Why should I stay out of it when I could make two people, one of whom I care about very much, happy?" I'm speaking of Victor, of course. Although I have to admit, after everything we went through this weekend, I have a renewed sense of respect for Phoebe Van Cleave.

"Who are you talking about?" Dad asks.

"Phoebe and Victor Marino," I say, waiting for the table to react.

"I thought I saw a certain something there," Brittany says. "Are you sure?"

"As sure as I was about you and Will."

Brittany flushes.

Mom clutches her chest. "I knew it!" She looks between Will and Brittany, and her face melts with happiness. "I've been waiting for this day forever."

"Not as long as me," Brittany says. Will shoots her a grin, and they share a secret smile that makes my heart sing.

Mom squeals like she's won the lottery. "I'm so happy! We have so much to look forward to in the coming months!"

"Oh, yeah, like what?" I ask.

Dad kicks Mom under the table. George McGuffin is a lot of things, but discreet isn't one of them.

"Nothing," Mom squeaks. "Forget I said anything."

Right. Obviously, my mother has a secret she's dying to share. No worries. Mom can't keep a secret to save her own life. By the end of the night or tomorrow at the latest, she'll be spilling the beans.

"That's not all that happened out on the island," Will says. "I have a confession to make."

Sebastian chuckles. "Here? At my parents' table?"

"Not that kind of confession. Look," he says, putting his napkin down on the table, "there's no easy way to say this, but you know J.W. Quicksilver, the guy who writes the espionage thrillers?"

Dad's eyes go wide. "Is he making an appearance at our library?"

"Wait until Betty Jean and the rest of her book club find out!" Mom says. "They're *obsessed* with him." What she left out is that Mom is obsessed with J.W. Quicksilver's books too.

"He's already made an appearance," Will says. "Actually, he makes an appearance every Monday through Friday, nine to five. Some Saturday mornings too."

Mom, Dad, and Jim looked confused. Sebastian meets my gaze with an approving nod. I suspect he's been trying to get Will to come out as J.W. Quicksilver for a while now.

Jim is the first one to catch on. "Will, are you saying *you're* J.W. Quicksilver?"

"Yep. That's me."

I don't think I've ever seen Molly McGuffin completely speechless before. Too bad I can't bottle this moment. Unfortunately, the moment only lasts so long. "Will Cunningham! I can't believe it. I mean, of course I can believe it—you're an extremely talented writer—but ... my goodness! J.W. Quicksilver," she says, dazed.

Everyone starts chiming in, congratulating Will and asking him questions all at the same time.

"What are you going to do now?" Sebastian asks.

"Tell the rest of my family and friends. Then I'm taking a leave from the library until I figure things out completely."

"So, Will," Dad says, "about your next book ..." Dad starts grilling Will on the plotline for the next book in his series, and Will good-naturedly goes along, answering questions about his characters and where he gets his ideas from.

Brittany starts to clear the table. "Lucy? Want to help me?" She motions toward the kitchen.

"Absolutely."

We grab all the dishes and head to the kitchen, where we close the door and immediately explode like a couple of teenagers who haven't spoken in over a week. "Can you believe it? Will and I are dating!"

"I always knew it was going to happen," I say.

She leans back against the counter, her brown eyes shining with happiness. "We ordered Chinese and talked for hours last night."

"So what's next?"

"Like Will said, he's going to take a leave of absence from the library. And then in two weeks, he's going to New York to visit his agent and his publisher." She smiles shyly. "And he's asked me to go with him. He says he's always admired my business sense and he wants my opinion on *everything.*"

"I guess that means you've completely forgiven him for keeping the J.W. Quicksilver thing a secret from you? You were pretty upset about it on the beach."

"I admit, I was upset, but I understand why he did it."

I struggle to keep my tone serious. "And you're all right with dating a world-famous author? As opposed to, you know, a grossly underpaid civil servant?"

She smiles breezily. "You know the old saying, Lucy; it's just as easy to fall in love with a rich man as a poor man."

Go, Brittany!

The door to the kitchen opens, and Travis comes in. "Sorry to interrupt, but can Lucy and I get some privacy?"

"I'd love to give you some privacy." Brittany blows me a kiss on her way out the door.

I brace myself for what's coming. Here's the part where Travis lectures me about how I'm always putting my life in danger, blah, blah, blah ... "I know what you're going to say."

"You do?"

"First, can I just tell you how handsome you look tonight?" I'm not just hoping to score brownie points with my compliment. Normally, Travis wears shorts or jeans to my parents' Sunday night dinner, but tonight he's wearing crisply ironed khaki slacks and a long-sleeved blue shirt that brings out the green in his eyes.

He seems rattled by my compliment. "Thanks. This is what I was going to wear to The Harbor House for dinner last night."

That again? He's harping on our missed date more than usual. I gulp. "I'm sorry about that. I really am. Maybe ... maybe Sarah and I can put off the new computer system and we can reschedule our dinner for next Saturday?"

He sighs heavily. "Lucy," he says, "I was going to save this for a better time and place, but I think it's best if I just get this over with."

I suck in a breath. "You're breaking up with me? In my *parents'* kitchen?"

He looks shaken. "What? No! I'm asking you to marry me."

"Marry you?"

That must have come out louder than I thought, because suddenly, the door bursts open and everyone starts piling into the kitchen.

"Did someone mention marriage?" my mother asks, looking on breathlessly.

Paco barks in excitement.

Travis looks resigned to the interruption. "I was just getting to that."

Jim clears his throat. "You're supposed to get down on your knees, son."

"Oh, yeah." Travis pulls a ring out of his shirt pocket and gets down on one knee. "Lucy, you're the stubbornest person I've ever met. You drive me crazy with all your schemes, and you're going to give me a heart attack and put me in the hospital one day. In spite of all that, I love you more every second we're together. Will you marry me?"

Now I'm the one who's speechless. Not because I don't love Travis and I don't want to marry him but because this was the last thing I was expecting tonight. I look at the hopeful faces of my family and friends, Paco and Ellie included.

I know what I want to say. I want to say *yes* with a capital *Y*. I want to jump into Travis's arms, and most of all, I want to try that ring on my finger because it's absolutely gorgeous.

Then a tiny voice in the back of my head warns me. What if Jenny is right? What if I lose my gift when I get married? What if I can never communicate with Paco again?

I've never not had my gift. And even though I've only had Paco for a year, and sure, we've almost been killed more times than I can count on one hand, this past year has been the best year of my life.

But it hasn't been the best year of my life because I've suddenly become an amateur detective. It's been the best year of my life because I met and fell in love with Travis Fontaine.

It's not hard to figure out the secret my mom and dad were whispering about at dinner tonight. Or why Mom suddenly wanted to get mani-pedis together. Travis is just old-fashioned enough that he would have sought their permission before asking me to marry him.

It's the little things like that that make him fit so well into my family. And the bigger things too—like accepting that I have this strange and sometimes wonderful gift, and then there's the fact that my dog and I can communicate with one another. There aren't a lot of guys on the planet who would believe it, let alone put up with it.

I struggle to speak past the growing lump in my throat. "Did you ask for permission first?"

"Um, well, I asked your parents, if that's what you mean."

"Not them."

He looks confused. For about a second. Then he gets it (which is just another reason he's the perfect man for me). With a sloppy grin on his face, he stands up and turns around to face my dog. "Paco," he says in a perfectly serious voice, "I'm in love with Lucy. I promise to always be good to her. And you too. You'll never want for any dog bones while I'm around, little guy. So, what do you say? Do you approve? Can I marry her?"

Paco barks and starts chasing his tail while doing a happy dance. *Yes!* Everyone laughs.

"Well?" Travis says to me. "Anything else I need to do?"

"No." His face falls. "I mean, no there's nothing more for you to do. *Yes!* Yes, I'll marry you. Now put that ring on my finger before you change your mind."

He slips the ring on my finger then lifts me up and twirls me around the kitchen while everyone claps. It's like something out of a fairy tale.

"Oh, Lucy!" Brittany says, sniffling with tears. "Who would have thought we would both be so happy?"

"Let's get out the champagne!" Dad says. "We've been keeping it cold ever since Travis came to talk to us." Mom runs to get the good flutes from her china cabinet. Dad pours everyone a glass, then makes a toast. "To Lucy and Travis!"

"To Lucy and Travis!" everyone echoes.

"To the wedding!" my mom says on the next round.

"To the wedding!" everyone shouts back.

"Speaking of weddings," Mom says, "I have an entire notebook with lots of ideas already."

"That's, um, great, Mom. I can't wait to see it."

"How about tomorrow morning? I'll swing by The Bistro, say ten? You always take a break about then."

"Well—"

"Lucy," she says sternly, "there's no time to waste. We'll need to book the church. Thank goodness we have an 'in' with your brother. But there's the venue for the reception and the flowers and ... I'm exhausted just thinking about it all!"

Travis catches my eye and winks.

So am I, Mom. So am I.

THE END

Books By Maggie March

Lucy McGuffin, Psychic Amateur Detective series

Beach Blanket Homicide

Whack The Mole

Murder By Muffin

Stranger Danger

Two Seances and a Funeral

The Great Diamond Caper

Dead and Deader

Castaway Corpse

My Big Fat Cursed Wedding (coming July 2023!)

Want to know when I have a new book out?

Subscribe to my newsletter at www.maggiemarch.com for all the

news!

About Maggie

Maggie March writes page-turning cozy mysteries filled with humor, unexpected twists, and a little dash of romance. Born in Cuba, she was raised on Florida's space coast, and spent three decades as a labor and delivery nurse before pursuing her passion for writing full-time. She and her husband of thirty-seven years and their 2 little dogs live in central Florida, where she enjoys the beach, going out to lunch with friends, and solving challenging crossword puzzles. She's also on a lifelong quest to discover the ultimate key lime pie recipe (but not the kind they served on Dexter!). With three grown children and an adorable granddaughter, Maggie knows there is nothing better than spending quality time with loved ones.

Maggie loves hearing from her readers. You can write to her at maggie@maggiemarch.com

Maggie also writes heart-warming small-town contemporary romance as her alter ego Maria Geraci.

Acknowledgments

Most of all, I'd like to thank my readers. Without you, there would be no Lucy McGuffin or any of the other zany characters who live inside my head. Thank you for allowing me to pursue my wildest dreams as a published author!

I'd like to thank my copyeditor, fellow author, and friend—Chris Kridler, who tries to keep all my commas straight. Any errors, typos, or other miscellaneous literary no-no's are strictly on me.

Thank you to Kim Killion for my fun covers.

And last but not least, to my better half, my sweet hubby of over 35 years, who always believed in me even when I didn't believe in myself.

Made in the USA
Coppell, TX
04 August 2023

19944664R00114